CLOUD DANCER

CLOUD DANCER

MARY ANN McGUIGAN

CHARLES SCRIBNER'S SONS
NEW YORK
Maxwell Macmillan Canada
Toronto
Maxwell Macmillan International
New York Oxford Singapore Sydney

Charles Scribner's Sons Books for Young Readers
Macmillan Publishing Company
866 Third Avenue, New York, NY 10022

Maxwell Macmillan Canada, Inc.
1200 Eglinton Avenue East, Suite 200
Don Mills, Ontario M3C 3N1

Macmillan Publishing Company is part of the
Maxwell Communication Group of Companies.

First edition   10 9 8 7 6 5 4 3 2 1
Printed in the United States of America

Library of Congress Cataloging-in-Publication Data
McGuigan, Mary Ann.
Cloud Dancer / by Mary Ann McGuigan. — 1st ed.
        p.   cm.
Summary: Making friends with Liz, a college student who sings in Lincoln Park, helps fourteen-year-old Eileen McDonaugh realize that she has the ability to face the various problems of her poor family.
ISBN 0-684-19632-8
[1. Family problems—Fiction.   2. Brothers and sisters—
Fiction.   3. Poverty—Fiction.]   I. Title.
PZ7.M47856C1 1994   [Fic]—dc20   93-5562

For Gil, Matthew, and Douglas,
who made room for my crazy dream

For Mama, Junie, and Eddie,
and for everything we shared

1

The envelope in the mail from Eileen's father had twenty dollars in it and a sentence scribbled on a cocktail napkin that still bore the impression of his glass. He wanted another visit.

It was late February. Cold. The snow on the sidewalks had been there and been there. Dirty layers marked the winter's passing like tree rings. Eileen McDonaugh and her big sister, Deirdre, and her little brother, Neal, trekked up the hill to the bus stop in so many layers of flannel and wool that they all but lost the use of their movable parts. Eileen's parents had separated last summer, but her father didn't ask to see them until December, so their visits were made in boots and leggings and scarves and hats and merciless layers of sweaters, each one donned obediently under the eye of the hawk— Deirdre.

The bus ride to their father's was an endurance test. The heat had one setting: intense. So for half an hour Neal and Eileen sat as close to the accordion doors as they could and prayed for someone to flag the bus down

1

or get off at the next stop so they could feel some air against their cheeks.

The visits weren't fun. They never laughed. They hardly spoke. He'd forget they were coming and answer the door wearing the undershirt he'd slept in. Later he'd peek over his sports pages to ask them how they were doing, so they'd make stuff up. They watched TV and he gave them popcorn, but not always. Sometimes he had licorice, and they'd dig out tiny bits of it from their cavities all the way home on the bus.

That day he took them to Gerrity's Tavern for hamburgers and potato chips. They had to walk several blocks down Kennedy Boulevard in the cold, wind ripping across the side streets. Eileen didn't mind the walk because they'd pass Sweet Notes, the music shop that had her guitar in the window—the guitar she'd wanted since the Fall Music Festival when Mr. Glatt, the music teacher, had chosen her from all the other eighth-graders in the chorus to sing solo. He'd practiced with her nearly every day, and nearly every time they practiced he'd told her she had a good strong voice, with professional potential, and that she should learn an instrument to accompany herself. The guitar was the most practical choice, he said.

Eileen ran ahead of the others to look in the window. The light against the glass turned it into a mirror. She hated mirrors, mostly because they were so uncompromising about what she looked like. Her hair was mousy brown, thick and straight, uncurlable and totally disobedient. Her eyes were green but small and sad. Everything about Eileen was small. She was already fourteen, sneaking into adolescence with the body of a ten-year-old. She touched her chin, exploring the pimple that had arrived that morning. It was going to be a big one. When there was no mirror around, Eileen could pretend her skin was smooth and her hair glorious. She brought her face closer to the window to see the guitar and be rid of her reflection.

Her father's giant silhouette came up behind her, with Deirdre and Neal beside him. He was very tall, though he never seemed to be standing his full height, always slouching or leaning. He had wide shoulders and the slim waist of a man half his age. Sometimes Eileen thought he was handsome, when he wasn't angry. "I bet you'd like to sing a song with that one on your knee," he said. He knew she would. It was no secret. Eileen told him how much she wanted it every chance she got. He put his hands into his trouser pockets and jingled his change. The wind took his graying hair this way and that, mocking the swagger of a pose he was trying so hard to strike. "Well, suppose I send your mother the money next week to buy it for you?" He glanced at Deirdre to see if he'd made an impression. But she was hard; Deirdre had no patience for fantasies.

They walked back down their block late that afternoon with a big orange sun setting in between the long shadows of the apartment houses at the bottom of the hill—at least Deirdre did. Eileen flew down, sliding behind Neal along every patch of ice. When they reached their building, Deirdre called after Eileen again, saying not to get her hopes up. But Eileen bolted up the five flights, tearing off layers as she climbed, and found her mother ironing in the kitchen. She couldn't get the words out fast enough. "Daddy's buying me the guitar. The guitar in Sweet Notes's window. He's sending the money next week." Her mother hardly caught a word, so Eileen told her again.

3

"Well, that's wonderful," her mother said, but she didn't seem to be listening; she was concentrating on a sleeve. Deirdre came in and gave her mom a look.

"That guitar is a hundred and fifty dollars," Deirdre said.

Eileen could see that Deirdre didn't believe he was buying any guitar. Neither of them did, and she was afraid they would jinx it before it had a chance to happen. Eileen left them, went into the bedroom. She took her leggings off, threw them into the corner, remembering too late that her ship was still in the pocket. He'd made it for her at the tavern, folded a paper napkin into a sailing ship, a toothpick for a mast. He'd put it on the bar when he was finished, told her it was magic, whispered in her ear. "This will take you anywhere you want to go," he said, and pushed it gently along the bar. Eileen stood eye level with it and watched it journey behind the bar's rim—a smooth, dark wave—to a spot where the stubborn early-afternoon sun had pushed itself through the tavern's tiny square window, a prisoner's cell of a window, and lit the fragile sail.

2

The first Sunday in March was a fairy day—the kind of warm bright morning that the little people bring when you least expect it. You walk outside in your winter coat, hardly paying attention to the world until you walk a ways and realize it's a day you haven't breathed or tasted in much too long.

After ten o'clock mass Eileen walked with her family to Lincoln Park, the streets busy with Sunday strollers. When they got there, Mrs. McDonaugh rested on a bench with Deirdre to watch the people go by. Eileen walked with Neal to the lake. People were playing, running, laying claim to the day. Neal ran ahead, stopping here and there to throw pebbles across the surface of the lake. When Eileen felt herself far enough away from her mother, she stopped by a tree, sank down, and lay back to watch the sky through the branches. They were still bare; no signs of life. She listened to the park, a young mother calling, a toddler giggling, the thump of a ball in a leather glove, bike wheels whizzing. But something didn't match, something nearby, voices arguing, not raised but angry. At least the girl's voice was. The guy was sure of himself, smooth. "I'll leave it on the bench. I will," the girl hissed at him.

"I need your help. It's the last time."

"I said no."

He didn't seem to hear her. "He'll have a Mets cap on."

Eileen turned to look at the couple. The girl looked like a college student. She was sitting on a bench by herself, a guitar on her lap. The guy was tall and blond, good-looking, moving away from her. "You'll be okay, babe," he said, then walked full stride up the lane toward the top of the park. The girl stood as if to follow, grasping the guitar, furious. "Phil," she called, but not as loud as she might have. She seemed not to want to call attention to herself.

She sank back down onto the bench, defeated. She was still for a second or two, then got up again, then down, at a loss for what to do about whatever was making her so angry. Finally, she pulled the guitar against her, strummed a hard, loud, angry chord, then another, settling into something, some kind of blues song. Once she started singing, Eileen recognized it. It was something by Bonnie Raitt. The girl sounded pretty good, and folks were stopping to listen a little, then putting dollars and quarters into the guitar case opened on the ground. The case was lined, as if it had wall-to-wall carpeting to keep the coins quiet when they landed, not to disturb her song.

Neal heard the music and lost interest in the lake. Eileen got up and they wormed their way to the front of the circle that had formed around the girl. The song had a good beat, and Neal started dancing. The crowd thought it was funny. Cute funny. The guitar player got a kick out of him, too. She called them over when she finished her song, asked them who they were.

"M-m-my name is Neal."

Eileen said nothing.

"Where'd you learn to dance like that, Neal?" Neal shrugged like it was a dumb question. He thought everybody danced. The crowd thinned out while they talked. The girl was friendly but seemed preoccupied, her mind on something else. "Is this your brother?" she said.

"Yes," Eileen said.

"How old is he?"

"Eight."

"I'm Liz," she said, but Eileen didn't respond.

"Does your sister have a name?" Liz said.

"D-d-dopey," Neal said.

Liz laughed. Eileen liked the way she laughed. She used any excuse to do it. It was not unexpected the way it was with her father. When her father laughed, Eileen worried because it meant he was either drunk or wanted to be. Liz laughed the way she breathed; it made her face red like her hair and her freckles. She had freckles everywhere, even on her eyelids, with eyes like pale blue planets in a galaxy of freckles.

"What else can you guys do?" she asked, seeming eager now for a distraction, something to keep her mind from what had just happened or was about to.

"M-m-m," Neal stuttered, and Liz watched him. Most people found something else to look at when Neal stuttered, but Liz didn't. She just waited, watched how hard he was trying, and it made Eileen wonder about her. Liz strummed a chord on her guitar and said, "Take your time, Neal." Neal had heard this before. Everybody said that when Neal talked. Especially his mother. But she said it as if the whole business was *her* problem instead of Neal's. Said it as if she'd given him the magic solution so why didn't he just slow down already and stop making her life miserable. Neal had the good sense to stop trying when his mother got like that. But Liz he believed. It didn't keep him from stuttering, but it kept him from clamming up.

"M-my sister can sing," Neal said.

"Can she sing as well as you dance?"

Neal shrugged.

"Let's hear you," Liz said, and gave Eileen an intro on the guitar.

Eileen shook her head no.

"Only onstage, eh?" Liz said, and crossed her long legs in front of her, leaned back against the bench. She was long and wiry, much stronger than she looked. She had a dancer's kind of body, always ready to spring, never meant to settle into one place for very long.

Eileen gave Liz a sullen look.

"I don't think your sister likes me."

"She d-d-don't like me either."

"Maybe it's my guitar playing she doesn't like."

"She c-c-can't play the guitar."

"I give lessons, you know. I could teach you how to play." Eileen shrugged. "Not interested?"

"I don't have a guitar."

"They don't cost that much. I know somebody selling one secondhand. You could probably get it for seventy-five dollars. I bet he'd even let you pay it off."

She said it as if seventy-five dollars were nothing, as if

people spent that kind of money to make themselves happy without blinking an eye. Eileen played along. "There's a guitar in Sweet Notes that my father's going to buy me."

"They give lessons there. At Sweet Notes. I worked for them last summer."

"G-g-giving lessons?"

"No. Dusting pianos mostly."

"You like playing here?" Eileen asked her.

She pointed to the money in the guitar case. "I'm saving for my retirement."

"You make a lot doing this?"

"Keeps me in strings." She leaned forward, looked down the lane, as if expecting someone, someone she didn't want to see.

"How come you don't get a regular job?"

"You mean like dusting pianos?"

"I hate to d-d-dust," Neal said.

"Me, too," said Liz. "Guess that's why they had to let me go. Shot a hole right through my retirement plan."

"You come here a lot? I mean to sing?" Eileen said.

"Every Sunday once it's warm. Sometimes Saturdays too. But you don't make as much on Saturdays. It's mostly fathers and kids. Sundays you get the moms after church, feeling good. That's when they like to be generous to types like me. Makes 'em feel like they're makin' a difference."

She looked down the lane again, stopped talking. She seemed to be watching someone approaching. He didn't look to Eileen like anyone special. Just a kid, maybe seventeen or eighteen, wearing a Mets cap. He took a seat on a bench a little bit away. Liz seemed upset, distracted.

9

She settled her guitar on her knee again. "Excuse me, folks, I gotta make some money." She did another song by Raitt, something about not wanting to be somebody's sugar mama no more. Eileen liked it. People were stopping again, a circle forming. The boy in the Mets cap joined it. Eileen had a chance to look at Liz more closely now that she was busy with her song. She didn't seem to be singing for the crowd, or even to be aware of them. It was as if she was inside herself somewhere, enjoying how the song made her feel. Eileen knew about that place where a song could take you, when the sounds you made, the just-right sounds, changed you into someone else, someone special.

When Liz finished, she thanked the crowd, gave them girlish smiles. She started fixing a string, and the people drifted away. "You sing real good," Eileen told her.

"Well, thank you, Miss Neal."

"Eileen. Eileen McGuire."

"Eileen. Hmm. Eileen." She made some funny sounds with the guitar, moving her fingers fast down the shank of it, and made a song with her name. "Eileen. Eileen. Lean and mean. Right, Neal?" she said.

"R-r-r, yeah."

"You two live around here?"

"On Magnolia," Eileen said. They lived on Bergen Avenue, nowhere near as nice as Magnolia. Neal didn't disagree. He'd heard Eileen do this before.

"Where d-d-do *you* live?"

Liz looked at Neal for a long moment, as if remembering something. "Wherever I can, mostly."

She looked over her shoulder, making sure there weren't too many people nearby. "Neal, get some of the dollars out of the case." She watched Neal remove the dollars and said to Eileen, "If you leave too much in there, they pass you by." Neal handed her the money. One of the bills was folded up tight and small, the one she slipped into her pocket. "Hey, Neal, we did real well. I bet it's 'cause of your Michael Jackson act, partner. Here," she said, tucking a single into Neal's shirt pocket, "you bring me luck." She slipped the rest of the money into her back pocket and got quiet again, nervous.

"What's the matter?" Neal said. He wanted her to talk some more. Eileen could tell Neal liked her already. She didn't answer, didn't seem to hear him, until he asked her again. This time she looked at him and seemed to find some kind of solution. "Neal," she said, "Neal, will you do something for me?"

"Sure."

"Take this over to that guy on the bench. The one with the Mets cap on." It was a little brown lunch bag, all wrinkled and soft as though it had been handled a lot. Neal seemed confused. "I can't leave my case," she said. "The money. You know. That guy left this at my friend's house. It belongs to him."

Neal looked over at the kid. He was back on the bench again. "Him?" he said. Liz nodded. Neal took the bag and darted the few yards. He was back in a matter of seconds, and the boy went away with the bag. Liz hadn't watched. She tightened a string, searched for the sound the chord should make. Neal sat on one side of her, Eileen on the other.

"D-d-did your husband throw you out?" Neal said.

"Neal . . . ," Eileen scolded.

Liz laughed. "I don't have a husband."

11

"Your m-m-mother kick you out?"

"In a manner of speaking." Liz began to strum something softly. "She treats me like a cat. But instead of putting me out at night, she puts me out in the morning and lets me sneak back in at night."

"How come she's mad at you?" said Eileen.

"She doesn't like what I do for a living."

"What d-d-do you do?"

"I go to Saint Peter's College. I'm a career student, actually."

"What's that mean?" Eileen said.

"It means she thinks I'm avoiding work."

"You can't g-g-graduate?"

"It's complicated."

"What's your major?"

"That's the complication. Last semester I almost went back to English, the one I started out with four years ago."

"Why'd you switch?"

"I wanted to be a physicist, study black holes and intergalactic resonance."

"So what happened?"

"Couldn't get past Copernicus. Switched to psychology. I have a natural bent for that kind of thing. People open up to me right away."

"So you're going to be a psychologist."

"Nope. I'd have too many friends and family needing freebies."

"So you switched?"

"To sociology. For a while. Then history."

"Is that where you are now?"

"No. Business management."

"What?"

"I'm going into management consulting."

"What's that?"

"Two parts blarney and one part suit. I've already got the blarney. Once I get the suit, I can open for business."

"What d-d-does a consultant do?"

"Ah, that's the beauty of it. Good consultants—I mean the ones who know their stuff—don't really *do* anything."

Eileen spotted Deirdre and her mother walking toward them from across the park and interrupted Liz to ask the time, as if she'd just remembered she was late. She didn't want Liz to see her next to Deirdre. She hated when people saw Deirdre for the first time. They'd always look kind of dumb for a second until they got accustomed to how beautiful she was, with her long dark hair and her olive skin that never got a pimple. And she was so tall. But worst of all—the absolutely most humiliating thing of all—was that she had breasts. Big ones. Something Eileen had come to believe was never going to happen for her. They were just not in the cards. She was convinced she'd be the only female in the history of the human race to reach adulthood with the chest of a twelve-year-old boy.

"Come on, Neal," she said. "We have to go."

"Why?" Neal said.

"We'll be late."

"F-f-for what?"

"Grandma's."

Neal rolled his eyes.

"So long. It was nice meeting you," Eileen said.

"Same here."

"Bye," said Neal as Eileen dragged him away.

"Hey, come see me again," Liz called. "I'm here every week."

13

3

Nothing came in the mail for the guitar the next day, but Eileen wasn't worried. She could wait another week for the guitar. Dinner was the immediate problem. Sometimes when Eileen's father didn't send money, her mother would come home from work with a few extra dollars. She was cashier at the State Theater, and they went there after school. Deirdre watched the movies over and over. Neal liked to run down the aisles, pounding echoes through the theater. Eileen sat in the glassed-in booth with her mother, watching the passersby brace themselves against the wind and listening to her snap the dollars for a customer's change. But she had no extra dollars this time.

This time it was Eileen's turn to go to Mr. Zeigler's delicatessen. They only went there when they needed groceries on credit. Eileen always peeked in through the glass door first to see if Zeigler had customers. If he had a lot, she'd wait outside with her mother's note clenched in her fist, her hands dug into her coat pockets. That night she gave up waiting for the right moment. She plunged in, head down, stomach knotted.

Mr. Zeigler's counter was unreasonably high. Coins slipped out of hands, clinking against the metal counter-top and sliding down the glass front of the showcase of kosher cold cuts and German potato salads. She reached up as close to the top of the counter as she could get, straining to keep her balance and her dignity. Zeigler took the note and clucked his tongue. He knew Eileen, knew what her note would say.

Zeigler fetched the items, muttering and complaining the whole time, handling the things roughly, his hands raw and red from the cold meats. He grumbled louder when-ever Eileen's mother put cupcakes on the list, something not really needed. Deirdre hated when her mother asked for cupcakes. She felt the same way Zeigler did about them.

Zeigler finally took a heavy paper bag, leaned over the counter, and began working his figures, the skinny stub of a pencil lost in the pads of his thick fingers. Its squared point made dark noisy numbers against the coarse paper, and for a time that was the only sound in the store—that and his muttering.

But then the entrance bell tinkled. It was Beth Cola-surdo and her father. Beth was in Eileen's class at school, although Eileen wasn't sure Beth knew it. They came to the counter just as Zeigler was about to get his account book. The book had a place on one of the highest shelves. He brought it down in a great fanfare of getting and reaching in step to a soliloquy that bemoaned deceitful deadbeats and the thankless work of grocership and the proper way they did things in the old country. Beth watched them. There sat this dusty courthouse of a book and the pathetic collection of ingredients for their supper that night, and Beth looked at Eileen as if this were some sordid, strange transaction.

Mr. Zeigler turned the cracked, yellowing pages until he came to McDonaugh. He took his time entering the figures into the ledger. As usual, he read Eileen the new total and reminded her to be sure and tell her mother how large it was getting. "I can't run this store on charity, you know. You people think you got everything coming to you. Well, that's not the way it is for the rest of us. The rest of us have to pay our way."

"Yes, Mr. Zeigler," Eileen said. He liked kids polite, and she was hungry.

Mr. Colasurdo was embarrassed. He took Beth to the back of the store and pretended to look for some cereal. Eileen watched them as Zeigler packed the groceries. It seemed to Eileen that they had important things to say to each other, funny things, because Beth laughed when he looked down at her. When Beth moved away from him to look at something, he noticed the hem of her coat was up in the back, so he reached down and fixed it for her. Eileen could tell he probably did that sort of thing all the time because Beth didn't even take much notice.

The rest of the week passed slowly for Eileen, with no word from her father. Saturday morning she waited on the stoop for the mail carrier. Sometimes he came as early as ten; she was outside by eight. She spotted him more than four blocks away. He must have had a lot of mail to deliver, because he took a long time inside each building. Then he got closer and Eileen realized that he wasn't the regular carrier. She saw him backtrack into a building he'd already covered. That's when she got nervous.

16

She was convinced this guy would lose the letter or put it into someone else's box or leave it in his bag or drop it down a sewer. Or what if he couldn't decipher the scribbled address? She couldn't take any chances. She said a hard Hail Mary, then conjured up a spell just to be on the safe side. She kept her eyes on him every second he was in view, and when he went inside a building she touched her thumbs to her pinkies, and under no circumstances did she blink. She knew it would work.

He finally walked up her stoop, with a thick rubber band twisted around a stack of envelopes and magazines for all the tenants. She didn't ask him if he had a letter for McDonaugh—she couldn't risk breaking the spell—so she just waited until he put the mail into all the boxes. She didn't even rush to the box when he was finished. She knew magic requires faith. She just walked confidently over to the box and looked through the slats. There it was, a short white envelope just like the ones he always used. She opened the box, saw her mother's name in his handwriting, and squealed all the way upstairs. Deirdre wanted to know where she'd been all morning. Eileen ignored her. She just wanted to show her mother the envelope, ask her to let Deirdre take her to Sweet Notes after lunch. Her mother had the radio on. She was getting ready for work. Eileen gave her the envelope. Deirdre came in behind Eileen and caught herself midnag to watch her mother open it. A ten-dollar bill was closed into half a page of the *Jersey Journal*. Nothing was in there for the guitar. No explanation. No apology.

Eileen bit her lip hard.

"Why'd you get your hopes up, Eileen?" said Mrs. McDonaugh. "You know what he's like."

17

Eileen didn't answer. She felt like crying.

"Maybe we could get you a new tape next week," her mother said.

"I knew he wasn't sending anything," said Deirdre.

"Be quiet, Deirdre," her mother told her, but she didn't disagree.

Eileen ran downstairs. She wanted to be back outside. She hated their apartment. The closeness of it gave no escape, no place to be yourself, to get out from under the feeling that wanting something—anything—was bad, selfish. She hated her family and how poor they were. But it wasn't just not having money; it was not having hope. They could never wish for anything or plan for anything because there was this silent, dismal agreement among all of them that nothing came easy, that there was no point in getting excited about tomorrow because it would take all the energy you had just to get done with the day.

Eileen thought of her father and his drunken lies. She hated herself for believing him. She could never figure out why she did. Over and over again he'd promise things—a movie, a book she wanted, the smallest things, a game of rummy—and when they didn't happen, the insult could never be protested or even acknowledged. She had to pretend that it didn't matter, that it didn't hurt.

Sometimes she tried not to hear the promises, keep herself from believing one more time. This was how Deirdre and her mother protected themselves. They had shells that nothing could penetrate. But Eileen had no shell. She wanted so many things. Things that other girls had without even asking. But there were ways to get things. And Eileen had learned some of them already. Ways that could get you into trouble. But the trouble

18

never lasted, at least not as long as the wanting did—the wanting never went away.

Deirdre found Eileen on the stairs, sat beside her on the step. Eileen already knew what Deirdre would say and she didn't want to hear it. There was a silence for a time; then Deirdre broke the tension.

"How could you be so dumb?"

"I practice," Eileen told her.

"He was never going to send the money. And even if by some miracle he was going to blow a hundred and fifty dollars on us, you think Mom would spend it on a guitar?"

"Why not?"

"Eileen, get real. Neal's sneakers are falling apart. Mom's out of blood pressure medicine and you think she's going to get a hundred and fifty dollars in the mail and spend it on a guitar? What planet are you from?"

"I want it, okay?" Eileen was nearly in tears. "I just want the guitar. What's wrong with wanting something?"

Deirdre rolled her eyes, turned her face away.

"It beats giving up on everything like you and Mom. You might as well lay down, 'cause you're dead already."

"Eileen, you see that garbage can?"

Eileen didn't answer.

"You see it?"

"All right. What about it?"

"No matter how much it might want to and no matter how hard it might try, that can is never going to get to be a car. So instead of kicking about it and rolling down the street like it had wheels, the can just stays put and does its job, taking the garbage. It makes a lot more sense."

"Maybe to you."

"I guess you'd rather roll down the street."

19

"You got it. Vroooom. Vroooom."

Deirdre laughed and shook her head. "Let me hear you peel out."

Eileen did her best, a squealing, screeching shrill of a pitch that only an adolescent girl can reach. She spooked a scruffy-looking bulldog on a chain, out for his morning stroll. The dog jerked the chain, and the tired, defeated-looking man on the other end of it cursed the dog and the girls and his wife for making him walk it. He tried to pull the dog back under control, but the dog was strong and determined to get to Eileen. The tug of war lasted only long enough for the angry animal to see that the giggling girls were not a threat to him or to his little master. Some fierce barking was enough to satisfy his honor.

But the tired little man had more to say. "I ought to let him bite your legs off. It would serve you right." He went on about respect and peace and quiet and a bunch of other big issues grown-ups spend so much time talking about, things that made Deirdre and Eileen laugh all the more. He finally gave up on educating them and went on his way. When he was out of earshot, Deirdre said, "I bet I know what *he* wants to be."

"What?"

"God."

"Nah. A Nazi guard. He'd like that better."

"Yeah. Especially the uniform."

"What about you? What do you want?" said Eileen.

Deirdre's face changed, and Eileen thought of last summer, when Deirdre's girlfriend invited her to stay down at the shore for a while. Deirdre had to say no. Mrs. McDonaugh needed her at home with Eileen and Neal. And the time they had to move in with their grandmother—all the way downtown to new schools—just when Deirdre had made the cheerleading squad. And the time before that, and the time before that. Deirdre was angry, and Eileen was sorry she'd asked such a question, because the moment was gone and they were rare to begin with. Deirdre was back to being the Hawk. There'd be no more joking, only guilt trips about chores and homework and not putting too much toothpaste on the brush.

Deirdre tied her shoelaces, then undid them and tied them again tightly with double loops. She stood up and tucked the back of her shirt into her jeans.

"What somebody wants has nothing to do with anything," she said, then hesitated, as if something else had occurred to her. "Maybe I just want to get out alive."

4

Eileen spent the rest of the morning trying to avoid everybody—especially Neal. He wanted her to read him the sports pages. Eileen would read them, but only when she was bored stiff and had run out of things to do. He only asked Eileen, never Deirdre or their mother. They didn't read it right. Neal liked the way Eileen read, with feeling, like a sportscaster. The behind-the-scenes stuff was what interested Eileen, the parts about drugs and salaries—but she wasn't much interested in the descriptions of the games, so she made a game of it for herself, trying different voices and inflections, one day a Southern lady of society, next time a gum-chewing Brooklyn waitress.

Reading the sports pages had been Eileen's idea to start with, but only because she couldn't stand reading the back of Neal's baseball cards for him anymore so she'd suggested the paper. He loved it and haunted her daily ever since.

So Eileen had gone to her school yard to hide for the morning, watched some kids play basketball, listened to them curse and talk dirty. When she got back to the apartment everyone had already eaten lunch and Deirdre was mad that Eileen hadn't helped out with any work around the apartment all morning.

When Eileen walked in Deirdre was clearing away the dishes from the table and Neal was agonizing over the last slug of milk that Deirdre and her mother were insisting he finish.

"Where were you all morning?" Deirdre said.

"None of your business."

Eileen sat down to lunch in her usual place at the table, then wished she'd stayed at the school yard and bummed candy from someone instead. It was hash again.

"Don't talk to your sister like that," said Mrs. McDonaugh. "She's been cleaning all morning while you were off God knows where."

"When you finish your lunch, put away the junk you left in the corner of our room."

"That's not junk. That's my project for science."

"Well, keep it on your side then, or shove it under the bed. I'm sick of looking at it."

"I want to know where you're going when you leave this house," said Mrs. McDonaugh. "You understand me?"

"This ain't a house."

"Don't you get smart with me."

"It's your turn to do the lunch dishes," said Deirdre.

"Can't. Promised Neal I'd read him the sports pages."

Neal brightened, took his milk down in a gulp, and ran to find the paper.

"Not till you're done," said Deirdre. She put the sponge down in front of Eileen's lunch plate, a nasty reminder of what waited in the sink. Eileen couldn't decide which was less appetizing.

In less than six minutes Eileen had finished her lunch, washed the dishes, and was downstairs looking for Neal. She didn't call his name because she was afraid Deirdre would hear her from the window and find one more chore for her to do before she could escape. Eileen found Neal sitting on the *Jersey Journal* in the alley, racing Matchbox cars along the side of the building with his friend Tony.

"You coming?" she said.

"C-c-coming where?" said Neal.

"The park."

"What ab-b-bout the p-p-paper?"

"I'll read it when we get there."

Neal got up, picked up his paper and his Matchbox cars, and followed her. Tony did the same. He was a short, round sort of kid. Eileen couldn't stand him. Whatever he'd eaten last was always stuck between his teeth and his pants were always stuck in the crack of his behind.

"This ain't no parade," Eileen said to him.

He got the hint and lumbered back into the alley.

"See you later," Neal called. Eileen was walking fast; Neal half ran to keep pace. He was used to being whisked away like this. Eileen did it whenever she had to get away from her mother and her sister. Sometimes he wouldn't know where they were going till they got there. Sometimes she'd rant and rave about their mother and threaten to run away, maybe even move back with her father. Neal knew this meant nothing. She was just as afraid of their father as he was. More often, like today, she'd describe the vengeance she'd reap on Deirdre if she had to listen to one more order. It was a mistake to interrupt Eileen's tirades, but Neal often made it.

"She ain't that b-b-bad," he said.

"Oh, shut up. What would *you* know?"

Neal said no more. A balanced view would not be tolerated. The entrance to the park was just across the street and Neal didn't want her to change her mind and send him home.

Eileen kept at it till they were well into the park. She picked a bench near the softball field, but she seemed preoccupied, looking for something. Neal promptly opened up to the day's sports, but Eileen was having none of it yet. "Can't you just forget your stupid sports for once?" She crossed her arms; she wanted to pout.

"You said."

"Yeah, yeah." She grabbed the paper, made a fuss about straightening it out and folding it back just right. Neal wasn't discouraged. He knew she'd settle into it.

"'Bulls Stay Hot.'"

"That's ab-b-bout last night's g-g-game," Neal said.

"'Ken Wexler scored six of his twenty-eight points in the final three minutes as the Bulls defeated the Celtics one-twenty to one-oh-five tonight. It was the fourth straight victory for the Bulls and the sixth consecutive defeat for the Celtics. Ron Johnson led the Bulls with a season high of thirty points, Mike Belsen scored . . .' Oh, Neal, do we *have* to do this? It's so boring." She put down the paper.

"You said."

"Why don't we look for that girl? Liz. You could dance if you want."

"You only c-c-came here to see her."

"That's not true," Eileen said, but it was. She had thought about the guitar lessons all week and since this morning she'd begun thinking about the guitar Liz's

25

friend wanted to sell. Deirdre was right about her father; he'd never send the money for the guitar. But the guitar Liz had talked about was seventy-five dollars cheaper. If she could get her mother to agree, they could pay it off little by little. She wouldn't have to tell Liz they had no money. She could tell her she was paying for it herself out of her allowance.

Neal took the paper and stared at the photos, kicked some pebbles away. He looked pretty gloomy and Eileen felt bad. The sky was filling with big rain clouds.

"Here. Gimme that." Eileen searched the page for something better. "Let's try this. 'Mazon Comes Out Slugging Again. Da Yankees' training camp zeemed normal enough today, vit business as usual.'" She read in Mr. Zeigler's German accent. Her voice was harsh and guttural, impatient and unkind. "'But at least von Yankee, Ron Mazon, vaz out of da lineup, shpending da day vit his attorney. Mazon vaz arrested las night at da local nightshpot afta a patron claimed Mazon slugged him afta an argument. This iss Mazon's zecont arrest for zettling arguments da easy vay.'"

When the first few raindrops hit the paper, Eileen ignored them. She was enjoying herself too much to stop. But in a moment, the drops were rapid and cold, the wind strong. "Here it comes," Eileen said. "We better run." She took part of the paper, held it above her head, and ran for the dugout in the softball field. Neal took the rest of the paper and hurried after her.

The dugout smelled of wet wood, and the air was cool and damp. Eileen liked it in there, all enclosed, the rain separating them like a transparent curtain from the ragtag field. The field looked bigger to Eileen from here than it did from outside the fence. First base was much farther away from home plate than she'd realized. Eileen settled back on the wooden bench, stretched her legs. Neal stood on it, reached up, and touched the low, slanted roof with his fingertips. Puddles were forming fast along the baselines, and paper things and plastic skipped across the infield. Then all at once the rain beat the roof in a pounding rush that silenced everything.

5

Eileen didn't hear Liz coming. She appeared from the corner of the dugout, leaping and landing inside like a crazed broad jumper run amok. She was cursing, wet to the bone and without a coat, lamenting in short, breathless bursts that she'd hardly made enough money to buy a shoelace.

When she saw them, she seemed pleased with the idea. "Jackson, my man," she said to Neal. "That play at third was brilliant." Neal laughed. Eileen waited to be noticed, but Liz didn't oblige at first. She talked to Neal about what a bad day she was having. So Eileen decided she hated her; when Liz said her name, she changed her mind.

"Eileen. How's things with you?"

Eileen shrugged. "No better, eh?" Liz said, snapping open her guitar case on her lap. "Life's just that way sometimes." She took a big soft cloth from the foot of the case and began to rub the surfaces of the guitar. "Rain came out of nowhere."

"You were playing?" Eileen said.

"*Playing* doesn't do justice to what I was doing for that little crowd. I was more than halfway into 'Words Get in the Way.' You know. Miami Sound Machine? I mean, I was making sounds you don't hear on Earth too often."

"So what happened?"

"That fainthearted mob left me there. Just 'cause of a little precipitation."

"Your guitar is so wet."

"I had to finish the tune. I always finish the tune." She put the guitar away, closed the case. "That your paper?"

"You w-w-want it?" said Neal.

"Just the sports."

Neal gave her the paper and Liz found what she wanted, gave her attention to the page. Neal sat down beside her. They were like people waiting for a bus.

"What are you reading?" Neal asked her.

"Ah, just this thing about the Bulls."

"C-c-could I hear it?"

Liz didn't understand what he meant at first.

"The story," Neal said.

"Oh, sorry, Neal. Were you reading this? Here, you take it." She held the paper out to Neal, but Neal did nothing, just looked at Eileen, then sank back into the bench.

"Neal wanted *you* to read it."

"You mean to him?"

There was a pause. "Yeah," Eileen said.

"How come?"

Eileen lowered her voice, talked the way you talk about things that embarrass you. "Well, you know. 'Cause of the way he talks."

"What *about* the way he talks?"

"He can't read too good."

"What does that have to do with knowing how to read?"

Eileen shrugged. Nobody in her family ever asked that question. Everyone just kind of assumed it was all connected, one big problem.

Liz spoke directly to Neal this time. "What grade are you in? Third?"

Neal shook his head no. He had been left back in first grade.

"He's in . . ."

"Let him talk," Liz told her.

Liz looked at Neal, waited for an answer.

"S-s-second."

"Aren't you learning how to read in school?"

"I'm in a s-s-special class for reading."

Liz seemed to have found her answer. "You mean where you match shapes in workbooks and look at picture words until the bell rings?"

Neal didn't answer. Liz was quiet. The rain was letting up and she looked out into the field. It seemed as if she had left them, and Eileen wondered if they should let her be by herself. Finally, she spoke real softly to Neal. "Listen, Neal, I was in special classes like that, too. Only it was because they said I couldn't concentrate. I was hyper. I just couldn't take their bullshit. Stuttering can't keep you from learning how to read. That's just their excuse for not teaching you."

Eileen watched Neal's face; his eyes opened wide as plates and she knew he was as surprised as she. Liz looked angry. Eileen knew she wasn't angry at them, but at some memory, at that place she'd just come back from.

30

"You still want to hear about the Bulls?"

Neal nodded.

"'In the third period, with eight points by Bill White, the Bulls pulled away by twenty points.'" Liz read eagerly, stopping to comment here and there, offering her assessment of the talent on the team. She was a real fan, knowledgeable, enthusiastic, and totally biased. Neal loved this kind of talk. He agreed earnestly, repeated sentiments he'd heard from broadcasters on TV, even offered thoughts of his own.

Eileen felt left out. This was not what she'd had in mind for their visit, but she didn't know how to make herself part of their little connection. She wasn't even sure why she wanted to. Sports bored her only slightly less than people who talked about it.

"'White's performance ended with an elbow in the teeth midway through the period and he went to the bench.' He should have had one in the teeth the other night when he was stinking up the place. 'Terry Paige was helped off the court after straining his left knee. . . .'"

"Did you see the article about Mason?" Eileen said. "He's in trouble again."

Liz looked up, surprised at her interest. "The guy's a bum. He'll burn out before the season's half done."

"Maybe not," Eileen said matter-of-factly, feigning a greater understanding than she had.

"You into baseball?" Liz asked.

"Some."

"She hates b-b-baseball," said Neal. "Sh-sh-she don't know anything about it." He didn't like this, getting squeezed out.

"What stuff do you know about, Leen?"

"Know about?"

"Yeah. What do you do for a living?"

"I go to school."

"Jefferson?"

"Yeah."

"Seventh grade?"

"Eighth."

"There's no future in that. I never see any ads for eighth-graders in the classifieds."

Eileen laughed.

"You gotta find another line of work. What kind of experience you have? What are your marketable skills?"

"Washing d-d-dishes," Neal said when Eileen didn't answer.

Liz shook her head. "Dish washing is not an upwardly mobile skill."

"I do the laundry."

Liz seemed hopeful now. "Chinese?"

"American."

Liz shook her head sadly.

"I cut my mother's hair sometimes, the parts she can't reach."

Liz was delighted with this news. "That's it! There's your answer. You do hair. We'll promote you with something military, a variation on a crew cut, but more like AstroTurf. Here's your tag line for the opening ad. 'Tired of being one of the crowd? Let Eileen mow you down.' I get twenty-five percent off the top as your management consultant, choreographer, and receptionist."

"What sh-sh-should we call it?"

"What, the business?"

"Yeah," Neal said.

"How about Bosco and Oz?"

"Who are *they*?" said Eileen.

"My dogs."

"How come you want to name it after your dogs?"

"First of all, they're smarter than we are and more ambitious. And second, if the business goes under, the IRS chases them instead of us."

"Where'd you get that idea?"

"Picked it up when I was an accounting major."

"Hey, look. The rain stopped," Liz said. "I gotta get back to work." She handed Neal the paper, saw his disappointment. "Can I ask you a favor, Jackson?" Eileen wondered what it could be. "Can you come with me and do some of your jiggin'? I'm hurting for income today."

Neal looked at Eileen. She shrugged indifference.

"Yeah, s-s-sure," Neal told her.

They found a bench not far from the dugout. The sky looked undecided. Very few people were around, but Liz began playing right away and Neal danced his dance, making the puddles part of his performance. Eileen wiped the bench with the "Day's Business News" section before she sat down. A few people came out of hiding, wandering over to hear the music now that the swings were wet and the fields filled with puddles. Liz switched to a Michael Jackson song and some girls clapped hands to the beat; Neal made moves like ones he'd seen on MTV. He was good. People smiled. Liz smiled, too, watching the dollars fall into the case even before the song ended.

When the song was done, the little crowd clapped and laughed, and Liz leaned over to count the winnings. "You keep this up, Jackson, and I'm gonna need investment counseling," she whispered.

"How much?" Neal said.

"One second." She counted the last of it. "Six-seventy-five, not counting the nickels and dimes."

"Wow," Neal said.

"We're on a roll here, but we're gonna lose them if we don't keep it going. What do you say, Leen?"

"What?"

"A song," she said, and played the beginning of something by Amy Grant. "You must know this one."

She did. Liz sang the first few lines. Then Eileen joined her. She sang the song the way she always sang songs, staring down at her shoes. But Liz skipped a chord to lift up her chin, did that twice till she made Eileen understand that she should look into Liz's face as they sang. That made the singing feel different, like ice-skating with somebody bigger holding her hand, trying things she'd be afraid to do on her own. More people stopped to hear them and to look. But the looking didn't make her feel funny the way she'd imagined it would. It made her feel better—warm all over, solid—like she was really there. She thought about what it was like to get her mother to look at her. Always when she spoke to her mother, she'd be tending to something else, something other than Eileen. The dishes, the laundry, a TV show.

Her mother had sung blues in small clubs in the Village as a girl. Whenever they were together with her mother's family, someone would get her mother to sing, and Eileen was amazed at how the song would relax her, take her out of her old worried self to a kinder place. Eileen cherished these times because her mother never sang around the house, not if anyone was home. Sneaking into the apartment, Eileen would sometimes catch the end of a sad song that would last only as long as she wasn't discovered.

When the song ended, the people clapped and Liz sang another with Eileen once she figured out which ones Eileen knew. When the people had wandered away, Liz put her guitar in Eileen's arms and showed her where to put her fingers on the frets so she could make the sounds. It hurt to hold the strings down tight, but the sound was worth it. Neal got bored with them and headed back onto the softball field. Eileen had the tune in her head and hummed it to herself, but she couldn't change chords fast enough to make it hang together.

Liz told her she was doing well; Eileen wanted to believe her.

"How much do they cost?"

"What?"

"Lessons."

"Oh. Ten dollars. For an hour. You interested?"

"It's my mother, really. She wants me to learn."

"It makes sense. With your voice."

Eileen wasn't sure she heard her right. She wanted to say thank you but thought it would sound conceited, as if she, too, believed she sang well.

"The guitar's not hard. It just takes practice. You'd catch on."

When Eileen didn't answer, Liz started to take the guitar away. "Could I try it one more time?" Eileen said.

"Sure." She placed Eileen's fingers again.

Liz left the bench, leaned over the guitar case to pick up the money. Eileen kept switching chords, from A to C as fast as she could.

"Not bad. Not bad," Liz said. Eileen thought she meant

her at first, not the money. She gathered it up, came back to the bench, took the crispest dollar, and held it out for Eileen to take, but she didn't. "You're gonna need a union card soon."

Eileen smiled, and Liz left her there with the guitar and trotted out to Neal on the field. Eileen kept trying. A to C, A to C. She watched Neal and Liz pitching the ball or running a base and saw how easy they were together, smooth. Graceful dancers for her uneven sound track.

6

"Nothing's ever enough for you kids. Where am I supposed to get the money for something like that?" Eileen tried to make herself small, stay out of the realm of her mother's complaints. "There's only so much I can do. But I can't seem to get you to understand that."

Eileen wanted to leave, but she knew that would upset her mother even more. She had to stay for the duration, till the tirade ended. So she slid herself down against the living room wall, sat very still on the thin carpet, tucked her hands under her knees, and contemplated the toes of her sneakers, the places where the rubber soles had come away from the canvas, the unreachable places where the dirt liked to settle.

"I work and work. Work all day, come home and take care of you. But still you want more. Well, I can't give it. That's all. I can't give it and I have a good mind to stop giving anything. You can go live with your father. See what kind of guitar lessons you get out of him."

Deirdre walked into the apartment. She'd heard her

mother from the floor below. Her mother started again, encouraged by the new audience. "This one wants guitar lessons. Do you believe it? And she thinks I can afford a guitar to go with it."

Eileen looked up long enough to see Deirdre roll her eyes. "But it's only seventy-five dollars. That's half the price of the one in Sweet Notes," Eileen said.

Her mother felt stronger now, more sure in her belief that what Eileen wanted was indefensible. Her mother went into the kitchen, continuing her lament. "Will you give it up already?" Deirdre said to Eileen. Eileen didn't answer; she rolled down her socks in steady, even movements. "Guitar lessons? You've got to be kidding." They heard the refrigerator door, the swoosh of a can of beer being opened. The girls looked at each other, acknowledging in the glance what the rest of the night would be. Some homogenized sitcom. Then another. A litany of their mother's hurts and complaints, then more of both until she fell asleep or perhaps an old movie took her mercifully somewhere else.

Eileen felt ashamed for asking and her sister's look confirmed it. Guitar lessons. What place did such things have here? Except to remind them of their misery, of how little they had. Eileen pictured how it would be if Beth Colasurdo asked her family for lessons, the family gathering to talk, to work out how to get the money, the parents excited about her wanting to learn. And she felt angry, ashamed of the family she was stuck with, a family that made wanting something a punishment instead of a joy. She felt herself starting to cry, and though she didn't make a sound, hardly moved, Deirdre could tell.

38

"God, Eileen," she said. "When is it going to sink in with you?"

Eileen left the apartment, stamped down the stairs to find Neal out front. She needed to get away again for a while—maybe take him to see their friend Vinny, the shoemaker. If they hurried, they could catch him as he was closing up the shop. Closing was their favorite time to go because he'd let them help. He liked the shoes perfectly aligned on the counter for the next day, toes even, in the order they'd arrived so he could fix them in the same order the next day. Eileen and Neal would check the tags, make sure the numbers hadn't gotten mixed up.

Eileen loved the way the unlikely companions looked lined up along the counter, the narrow ladies' pumps next to the steel-toed work boots with dirty creases in their huge tongues, the tired wing tips with run-down heels, having to visit one more city, a pair of white patent-leather First Communion shoes, hunting boots, all of them side by side, at attention on the counter, all bearing the creases and bulges of their owners' feet, a still life of motion, the silent story of where they'd been and who they were. Always Eileen would find a pair with sides widened beyond anything the shoes should have been expected to bear. Surely Cinderella's sister's. The backs of another would be rubbed raw, curled inward, and Eileen would imagine an angry, hurried wearer, impatient with the need for them.

Eileen didn't sense that Vinny recognized the shoes' identities. They were a daily, changing, repeating assembly line of needy heels and soles. He liked them, Eileen saw, but showed no favoritism. Each would have a turn.

Vinny worked slowly. He did everything slowly. He was huge. People said his brain was addled, that there was something not right about him. Eileen's mother insisted he was dangerous, and they were forbidden to go to the shoemaker's shop alone. But Neal and Eileen had long ago shot enough holes in that theory to satisfy themselves that it was all wrong. Vinny was harmless.

Eileen and Neal had found him and his shop the day after they moved into the neighborhood. Eileen dared Neal to sneak into the shop, knock down the shoes on the counter, and run. He did it, and did it again and again week after week until they were so good at it that the sport was gone. The friendship started the day they got careless. Always, Vinny had come to the door as they ran and made a terrible sound at them, some kind of yell unlike anything they'd ever heard.

But one time, that last time, he didn't come to the door. There was nothing. So they slowed down halfway up the block, looked at each other, curious, then turned around, and with slow careful steps moved back toward the shop. At the entrance they saw the shoes on the floor, but the huge dark-haired owner was nowhere in sight. They hesitated, listened to the silence, then held their breath and stepped inside. Before they could hear themselves scream, Vinny came out from behind the door and slammed it closed. The entry bell, unaccustomed to such rudeness, clanged in protest. Eileen felt her chest tighten; she couldn't breathe. Vinny was big, and she realized that if half of what her mother had said was true, they were in serious danger. She pulled Neal close to her side, ready to defend, but the look on Vinny's face didn't make sense.

40

He was sad. That's all. Sad. Not angry or mean. She saw that he knew they were frightened.

He raised his huge hand, as if to calm them. "Shoes," he said. "You pick up." Eileen decided that if a hippopotamus had something to say, he would sound like Vinny, a thick, deep voice, bigger than its own mouth. Neal, eager to please, began to throw the shoes on the counter any which way. "No," Vinny said. "Numbers. I show." And he showed them the tags in each left shoe and how he liked them arranged on the counter. Ever since then, Neal and Eileen had spent afternoons with Vinny, especially if Deirdre was out baby-sitting.

Vinny had already locked the door when they arrived, but they pressed their noses to the glass and he let them in. He was finished with his closing rituals, ready to head to his back room, the tiny square place separated from the shop by a thin accordion door coming away from its track so that it looked as if it were holding back an unending hurricane. The room held his cot and his collection of model airplanes. Neal loved his supersonic military jets, especially the Phantom that moved at fifteen hundred miles an hour, and the big wide British bombers from World War II, with four propellers on each wing. Eileen liked the one that looked like the Red Baron's from the First World War. Many times she had watched Vinny work. She loved to see his big hands addressing the tiny, intricate parts, his lumbering motions managing such delicate tasks.

He was happy to see them, wanted to show them what he was working on. "Attack helicopter," he said.

"I love it, Vinny," Eileen told him. She sat on the edge of his cot. Neal took the floor.

"N-n-neat," Neal said.

"Let's take Cloud Dancer to the park, Vinny," Eileen said. Cloud Dancer was a huge towline glider plane with a six-foot wingspan and a balsa-wood body that Vinny had painted with big fluffy clouds on a sky blue background.

Vinny looked puzzled. This wasn't the time of day they usually took Cloud Dancer out.

"It's almost d-d-dark," said Neal.

"So, good," Eileen said. "Nobody else will be there. We'll have the whole sky to ourselves." She stood up, pulled Neal to his feet. "Let's go." They got to the hurricane door in a step or two, but Vinny wasn't following.

"Come on, Vinny. Get Cloud Dancer down." The glider hung from the ceiling on metal hooks.

"No," Vinny said. "Dark."

"Don't say no," Eileen pleaded, and Vinny could see that this was important, this was something she needed from him. Vinny, though confused by many things that many people did and said, understood what that meant. And he was always able to give.

By the time they got to the park, one side of the sky had pink and orange stripes in it, and Vinny aimed Cloud Dancer into that side of the night. There was a light wind and they headed into it. Eileen watched him work the tow-line, coaxing the plane to let the air embrace it. His shirt filled with air and his loose trousers clung to his legs as Neal ran ahead of him, eyes glued to the graceful craft, shouting traffic controller's orders. "You are c-c-cleared for takeoff, C-C-C-Cloud Dancer."

The plane finally took the air, and Vinny passed the line to Neal so he could be the one to let it go. The change made the plane jerk as if uncertain whether to break away. Eileen stopped running and watched the light from the day's end on the wings. Neal's giggles and Vinny's big laughter mixed as the two got smaller and smaller and harder to see and the plane got higher, seeking currents in the air, and she knew Neal must have released the towline and that Cloud Dancer was free.

7

Eileen slept late on Sunday. She had fallen asleep picturing herself playing the guitar with Liz, singing songs with her to cheering crowds like Kate and Anna McGarrigle, word spreading throughout Jersey City of their terrific harmony until they were in such demand that she had to leave her family to tour the country with Liz, playing at colleges and folk festivals, meeting fans and signing autographs. Her last thoughts before sleep were of Beth Colasurdo and her father sending two dozen roses to her dressing room after the performance, with a note begging for a solo performance or maybe just a few moments of her time.

She opened her eyes, then shut them quickly, pulled the covers over her head. Sunshine filled the little room. Deirdre had pulled the shade all the way up, her favorite way of punishing late sleepers.

Facedown in her pillow, Eileen pulled her knees up under her chest and let the blood flow to her brain. She believed this position helped her think through problems and often used it. Her biggest problem right now was how she was going to get the money to buy the guitar. In her mind, it was settled. She was *going* to have a guitar. Period. She'd just have to get the money somehow. She considered her father again, about asking him for at least part of it. No use. He was a dead end. She'd have to get a job, earn the money herself. Delivering newspapers? That didn't pay enough. Baby-sitting? The money was too unpredictable and she hated it anyway. Maybe she could help Vinny in his store. Forget it. He was as poor as a church mouse. Just when she thought she'd put the solution off till later, the craziest idea popped into her head. Electrified, she whirled herself up to get out of bed but got her legs caught in the covers and fell out instead. She lay flat on her back, smiling at the ceiling. Zeigler. She'd work for Zeigler. It was settled.

From the kitchen she heard her mother yelling at Neal, something about never remembering to take the garbage out. Eileen guessed she wasn't in too bad a mood. She never yelled when she was in a *real* bad mood. She stayed out of everybody's way. She'd probably want to go to mass. A real bad mood meant she wouldn't go. A little bad meant she would. So they'd all have to go together. Eileen decided she'd escape with Neal to the park as soon as mass was over.

Her mother was still picking on Neal when Eileen finished getting dressed and came into the kitchen. Neal had shut down. He was looking out the window, trying to get himself on the other side of the glass. Mrs. McDonaugh had her hands on her hips. "Do you hear me talking to you? Do you hear me?" She spotted Eileen and decided how to end this. "Eileen. What's the matter with him?" *You*, Eileen thought but dared not say it. "Go with your

45

sister to church," she said to Neal. "If you hurry, you can make the eleven."

They were out of the house like a shot. Eileen told Neal they would skip the church part and go directly to the park. They made it there in no time. It was nearly as crowded as it had been when they met Liz, but it was colder and Eileen was glad about it because she could keep her spring jacket on, one of the few things she owned that wasn't patched or frayed or pilled with age. That was always the meanest thing about Sunday, the day when everyone looked special. It made Eileen feel so much worse about herself because she had no camouflage.

They found Liz easily, on the same bench where they'd first met her. She was nervous, edgy again, said contributions weren't going very well. She moved a Shop-Rite plastic bag from the bench to the ground by her feet and motioned for them to sit beside her. Neal sat down close to her, no happier than when he'd left the apartment, but seeming content to be near her.

"I was hoping you'd come," she said, mostly to Neal. Neal wouldn't talk. He took a tiny man out of his jacket: G.I. Joe. Liz left him alone for a while then asked him if the man had a name, but Neal couldn't get the words out to answer her. He tried, but his face contorted and his body heaved until he finally gave up.

"He gets like that sometimes."

"Like what?"

"Can't talk at all."

"What's the matter, Neal?"

"He won't answer."

Liz didn't mind. "I have days like that. Days I'd like to

shut everybody out. Everybody." Neal glanced at her, then turned to his man again.

"It's not like he doesn't *want* to talk. He *can't,*" said Eileen.

"How do you know?"

"Well, my mother says . . ."

"Hey, Neal. What's the deal? You can't talk or you won't?" Neal didn't look at them.

"Seems to me your brother's pissed about something. He'll talk once he's figured out what he wants to say about it. Your brother's got the right attitude about words. Most people just throw 'em around like there was plenty more where that came from. Not Neal. Neal's got respect for words, like a writer or a poet. Right, Neal?" Neal looked up again, seemed less interested in his man. "Of course, that's probably because of how hard it is for Neal to say what he's got to say. I mean when he stutters."

Eileen looked at Neal. He met her eyes for only a second, time enough to acknowledge the shame. No one ever said that word around Neal. No one gave a name to it. That was forbidden. Eileen never knew the reasons for this; she only felt them—the awkward looking away, the pretending it wasn't there.

Liz sensed their discomfort, started to speak, then stopped. She seemed edgy again, now that there was nothing to talk about. It was as if something else was on her mind, something urgent she wanted to ask. She began to speak, then stopped, then tried again, finally coming out with it, making an effort to sound casual. "Feel like taking a walk, Neal?"

"Want to g-g-get rid of me?"

"No. I was just wondering if you'd take this bag over to

47

my friend." Liz turned slightly in the direction of the lake behind them. "See her? By the water, with the dog. The black dog."

"Yes."

"She forgot her bag." Neal looked unconvinced. "She was here with me before and left it. Would you give it to her?"

Neal looked at Eileen, as if wondering if she believed any of this. Her look told him she didn't. Neal shrugged, took the bag, and moved toward the girl and the dog. Liz turned back to her guitar; Eileen watched Neal.

"There are three million people in this country who stutter," Liz said. "Did you know that?" Eileen was surprised. "Nine hundred thousand of them are kids. And most of them are boys."

Eileen had no idea that so many people stuttered, but she did know they were mostly boys. She had read a little about it. "How come mostly boys?" she said.

"Nobody knows. Has something to do with the parts that get worked up when you're nervous."

"Parts?"

"When people get nervous, they feel it in different parts of their bodies. Some people feel it in their stomachs. Some get a rash. People like Neal tighten up the muscles around their mouth and throat. That's how come they have trouble talking."

"My mom says he'll outgrow it."

"You can't outgrow it. But you can learn how not to do it."

"Not to stutter?" Eileen whispered.

"Right."

"You mean speech therapy? None of that stuff works."

"It works. I know a therapist at the college. She helped my friend Chris. She's really good."

Eileen was getting uncomfortable. To her, Neal's stuttering was a neon sign declaring that something was wrong with their family. She didn't want to talk about it. She couldn't believe that Liz understood how bad Neal's problem really was. They were quiet for a moment. Eileen watched Neal make his way back to them. He said nothing when he reached them, just sat down on the grass with his little man, moving the figure's arms up and down as if the enemy might be near.

"You know, I'm not sure I like the guitar in Sweet Notes," Eileen said.

"Why not?" Liz said. "It's a good one."

"Maybe the one from your friend would be just as good."

"It'd be cheaper."

"And I could use the money left over to get lessons."

"Now you're talking."

Neal came over to them at the bench, looked at Eileen like she was crazy.

"You got any friends who want lessons?" Liz said.

"Maybe. I could ask around."

"You'd learn quick."

"Are you sure your friend wants to sell it?"

"You mean the guitar?"

"Yeah."

"You c-c-can't get a guitar."

Eileen kicked Neal's foot to shut him up.

49

"I was thinking about paying for it myself. Out of my allowance, I mean."

"What al-l-l-l—" Eileen pinched him this time, hard. Neal got the message.

"If you're interested, I'll talk to my friend," Liz said.

"Okay, ask him about it."

"I'll see him tonight. Call me and I'll let you know what he says."

"I better go." It was nearly twelve, and her mother would expect them home before she left for the twelve-thirty mass.

Eileen motioned to Neal and they said good-bye, then walked back up the black asphalt path lined with benches crowded with old ladies, past their blank stares as they watched them go by, another girl, another boy, nothing in particular. When she was a little bit away, Eileen turned around to see Liz. She was playing again, people stopping, and Eileen was afraid for a moment that it would all end here, with her looking back and Liz forgetting her. She left Neal in the path, ran back to the bench.

"Liz," she called, panicky. "I don't have your number." Liz stopped playing, looked puzzled. "Your phone number. I don't have it."

Liz reached into her bag for a pen. "Got a piece of paper?" she asked her.

"No," Eileen said, feeling stupid.

Liz asked the people around the bench. A guy tore a sheet of paper for her from a small spiral pad. She wrote something down quickly. "Here. That's my number. You can call me."

"I can call you," Eileen repeated, robotlike.

Liz laughed. "You can call me."

By Tuesday Eileen's mom had no money again, and it was Eileen's turn to take a note to Zeigler's deli. She was glad because by then she was ready to ask Zeigler for a job. She figured the old man was so crazy about hard work he'd never refuse. And his wife, Rose, complained all the time that she couldn't get on the ladder to stock the higher shelves. She couldn't move anything heavy. She simply couldn't keep up with things as well as she used to, and it was starting to show. Fingerprints stayed longer on the glass cases now. Cans got dusty on the shelves, things Rose never allowed before.

Rose and Mr. Zeigler were arguing when Eileen entered, and she was glad of it. It kept Zeigler's mind off the sins of the McDonaughs. When Zeigler started to pack Eileen's groceries, Rose left for the back room, weary of the old man's stubbornness. The groceries got the brunt of his final complaints. Eileen watched Zeigler reposition the heavier items at the bottom of the bag. She said the words to herself one more time, the words she'd practiced over and over. "Mr. Zeigler," she said. He didn't hear her. He was still talking to the groceries. "Mr. Zeigler," she said. This time he heard her and looked both surprised and slightly annoyed at her voice.

"What is it, girl?" She couldn't tell him. "Speak up," he said. "What did you forget?"

"I want to work for you." It didn't come out the way she'd practiced it. He just looked at her, confused. "A job, I mean. I want to have a job."

"A job!" he said.

"With you. Here."

"What are you talking?" He went back to packing the groceries.

"I can work hard. I can clean up. Unpack your deliveries, put them on the shelves."

"What are you talking? A job." He pushed the bag toward her.

"I can do a lot."

"You're ten years old. What kind of job for a ten-year-old?"

"I'm fourteen, Mr. Zeigler. I'm small for my age. Ask anybody."

"You're no good to me," he said, brushing her aside.

"I watch how you and Rose work the store. I can do anything."

He paused, looked at her, then seemed to dismiss the idea. "You couldn't even reach the shelves."

"I'm the tallest girl in my class, Mr. Zeigler. I'm the tallest boy too. I mean I'm taller than any of them."

"Small for your age and the tallest in your class."

"I've had ballet lessons. I can stand on the tips of my toes for hours."

He laughed, sounded like a walrus gargling, and said nothing for what seemed like a long time.

"You've got a bike?" he asked her.

"Oh, yes," she said.

"With a basket?"

Eileen didn't know how to answer because she couldn't understand his German accent. It sounded to Eileen as if he had said "mid-Nebraska," and she was sure Mr. Zeigler didn't deliver that far.

"A basket," he said, motioning with his hands. Eileen

knew what he meant then but didn't know what to say; she had no basket, didn't even know anybody who had one.

Mr. Zeigler laughed because he could see how badly she wanted a job.

"I got basket. It's okay. You come tomorrow after school, stay till we close," he told her.

Eileen smiled. He didn't smile back. "Thank you, Mr. Zeigler." She pulled the grocery bag to her side of the counter, hugging it to her. She turned away with it and headed for the door.

"Wait," he called. "How much you paid?"

She didn't know how much to ask for.

"Twenty dollars a week," he said, and went back to his work.

"Thirty," she said.

He turned, rolled his eyes. "Four days a week," he said.

"Three," she corrected.

He harrumphed, "You be on time."

Outside, Eileen half skipped, half ran up the block, thrilled with what she had done, picturing how she'd tell Liz she could have the lessons and buy the guitar, wondering how she'd ever find a bike.

8

The dollars were snug in the pocket of her jeans, rolled into a cylinder buried deep at the bottom where they couldn't possibly get out. Still, every few steps, as she got closer to Liz's bench, Eileen touched her pocket to be sure of them. She had never had this many dollars before and the idea that she was about to spend them on herself—on something she wanted more than anything else in the world—made her feel dizzy. She touched the money again to be sure it was really happening.

She'd worked for Zeigler two days that week. She hadn't found a bike, so she'd delivered the groceries on foot, carrying them in her mother's old shopping cart. When the week was over, Mr. Zeigler had paid her twenty dollars for the two days as promised and told her she could use his bike, said he was happy with her. Customers were pleased. She'd helped Mrs. Sullivan unpack her order and put the things away and gotten a tip for it. Eileen was confused at first, thinking the money belonged to Zeigler, until Mrs. Sullivan said, "You buy yourself some ice cream. You're a dear." She'd earned five dollars in tips.

She hadn't told her mother about the job yet because she knew she'd have to lie about how much Zeigler paid her. How else could she explain where the rest of the money was going? But she'd have to tell her mother soon. Deirdre was getting suspicious about why she wasn't coming home after school. She didn't believe Eileen was helping her teacher mark papers. But Eileen had decided it would be easier to tell her mother with money in her hand. She had fifteen dollars saved for her.

She heard Liz before she saw her. Liz was singing something Eileen didn't know. It was pretty, about soldiers dying for a cause. Liz told her later it was Irish.

"Are you Irish?" Eileen asked her.

"Most of me is. You too?"

"Yeah. My last name is McGuire."

"You must know some Irish songs, then."

"Some."

"Wanna sing 'em with me? You've got the voice for it."

"Yeah, that's why I came today."

"To sing Irish songs?"

"The lessons. I came about the lessons."

"Oh. The guitar lessons. Sure. Did you bring your guitar?"

"No, I decided not to get that one in Sweet Notes, remember?" Eileen looked down at her sneakers. "I thought it might be a better idea to get the one your friend is selling."

"Oh, that's right. But weren't you supposed to call me? I talked to Phil about you last week. He wants a hundred dollars, but I have a feeling he'll take less."

"Yeah, I was thinking about it. I couldn't decide. You see my mother wants to buy me a new guitar, but I told her I didn't want her annoyed at me if it turned out that I got bored with the whole thing—I mean, once we get started—so I told her we're better off getting the second-hand one you talked about. Anyway, then she may let me get the new bike I want."

"Great," Liz said. "I can stop by Phil's tomorrow night and get it."

"Well, I don't exactly have all the money yet." Liz looked confused. "I want to pay for this myself. Out of my allowance, I mean. You know, little by little."

"How little?"

"Five dollars?"

"I can talk to him about it."

It didn't look as certain as it had before. What if Phil wanted all the money at once? And even if he let her pay it off, it would take her forever. She had to give her mother at least fifteen dollars a week, and the lessons cost ten dollars. That left only five dollars for the guitar. It would take more than three months. The guy would never agree to that. Her stomach tightened. "No big deal," Eileen said. Liz waited, watched her rub her palm against her pocket. Eileen's face had closed up; the excitement was gone.

"If he wants the cash, you could always ask your mother."

"No," Eileen said. "It's no big deal. Forget about my mother."

"She on your case? I know all about that stuff." She palmed the crown of Eileen's head, gave her a shake. "Don't worry, we'll work something out."

She said it so easy, so casual, as if all things were possible. She talked like someone who could make things happen.

"I could give him a down payment," Eileen said.

"How much have you got?"

"Ten."

"Okay. Give me the ten. I won't see him tonight, but I'll stop by his house tomorrow night. Give me your phone number. I'll call you, let you know what he says."

"No. I'll call you," Eileen said. No one ever got to the phone before Deirdre, and Eileen did not want to have to do any explaining.

Liz shook her head. "Whatever you say."

"Tomorrow night."

"Tomorrow night."

Eileen dug the bills out of her pocket, handed them to Liz in a tight roll. She'd already separated the money for her mom. Liz peeled the bills apart, counted out ten soft, old singles. "Have you got a pencil? I'll give you my number," she said.

"I've got your number. I got it last time."

"All right, then, partner. Call me tomorrow night."

Liz gathered up the dollars and coins from her guitar case, put the bills neatly with the money from Eileen, and put the coins in a leather pouch. There were a lot of coins, and they made noise in the pouch until she pulled it closed with a drawstring, then put it in the pocket of her jacket.

She began to put the guitar away. "Where's Neal today?"

"Boy Scouts." The words just popped into Eileen's head. It sounded like something boys from normal families did.

"On a Saturday?"

"It's a special project."

Liz left it alone, didn't ask any more questions, just looked at her more closely, and Eileen looked away because she was afraid Liz knew something about her, something no one should know.

"Is Neal getting therapy?" Liz asked.

Eileen knew what she meant but pretended she didn't.

"Is somebody helping him with his speech?"

"No," she said.

Liz looked at her, and Eileen feared again that Liz might have figured out the kind of family she came from. "Oh, my mother's very concerned about him, though," she said. "She's looking into several places to get help."

"Oh. Okay, good." Liz went back to the guitar, and Eileen was relieved. Neal's stuttering was a dead-end topic with her mother. Almost a year ago, Eileen had gone to the library and gotten books about stuttering, books that had exercises, ways to help Neal get his words out. She had shown them to her mother, described the people the books talked about who had overcome almost all their stuttering. But the subject loosed a terrible anger in her mother, a rush of resentment. She had not neglected Neal. What could she do if they were never in a school system long enough to get things under way? She was tired, doing the best she could. The rush finally settled into the long, familiar tale of how Neal had been born so sickly and how the doctors breathed life into him. "He's lucky to be alive," she said. That's the way she ended every lament about Neal. "He'll never be Churchill, but he's alive."

Eileen had tried doing the exercises with Neal on the

sneak, but they didn't work the way the books said they would, and Neal wanted no part of them.

"I've read a lot about it myself," Eileen said.

"Yeah? There's a professor on staff who's into it. A therapist. She's the one who helped my friend."

"Yeah," Eileen said, wishing she would drop it.

"She helped me with my voice, too. For singing. She has a good book out about it."

"About singing?"

"No, stuttering."

"Oh." Eileen didn't want to hear any more. All Liz could see was what was on the surface. Neal needed help and there was someone who could help him. Easy. Except nothing was ever easy with the McDonaughs. Eileen reached for her jacket.

"Not your favorite subject, eh?"

"It's no big deal."

"I thought you'd like to see the book, that's all."

Eileen couldn't answer this time.

"Did I upset you?" Liz said. "I'm sorry."

Eileen swallowed hard, got her voice back. "Who's upset? What are you talking about?"

"Why don't you talk to her yourself? Her name is Margolin. She's real nice. Take Neal with you."

The idea of marching Neal into a therapist's office without her mother knowing was beyond anything even Eileen was willing to try. Liz could see she wasn't enthusiastic. "I've got an idea," she said. "Why don't I take you there? I could introduce you."

"Oh, no. That's all right. My mother and father can take him. Like I said, they're looking into the best way to help him."

"Yeah," Liz said, but she seemed unconvinced. Eileen wished this whole stuttering business had never come up. There was nothing *she* could do about it anyway. It was just something nobody was allowed to talk about in her family, like all the drinking. There was no way Liz could ever understand that, and Eileen was angry with her now, wished she'd just leave her alone about it.

"You coming around the park tomorrow?"

"Don't know." Eileen had it planned for noon.

"It's Palm Sunday, you know. That means a big crowd. A lot of money. I could use some help. Tell Neal I'd really like him to come, would you?"

Eileen thought she meant *her* help. She knelt down, pretended she had to tie her sneaker. "Sure," she said, then told Liz she had to run, she was late for a friend. She shuddered at what Liz would think if she knew the friend was a six-foot-four shoemaker with mostly dried-up brain cells.

9

When Eileen woke on Palm Sunday morning, Deirdre was still asleep. Thinking it had to be early, Eileen rolled over, mushed her face into her pillow to recapture her dream, but it wouldn't come back and she was feeling hungry. She got out of bed as quietly as she could; no point in making Deirdre part of things any sooner than necessary. Eileen impressed herself with how stealthily she opened the door; she heard her mother in the kitchen, singing, her voice soft and deep. Eileen knew the old song. "Stormy Weather."

She closed the bedroom door behind her and settled herself down onto the hallway floor. If her mother knew she was there, she'd stop singing. And Eileen wanted to hear. She closed her eyes, listened to what her mother did with the words, the lovely unpredictable way she'd lift them up, then down, then back to the song's simple melody. It was so delicious to hear this. This was a mother unlike her mother, not a victim, not angry, but gifted, confident, victorious. She imagined her onstage, in a spotlight, a long black glimmering dress, people dreaming to her song.

Her mother finished, and Eileen waited for another, but nothing came. Her mother's voice came again, talking this time. To her plants. Eileen got up, went to the kitchen. Her mother was reaching up, trimming a great philodendron that hung from the ceiling. "Come here. Look at this," her mother said. She seldom bothered with hellos. She'd lost the need to mark beginnings.

Eileen came to her mother, followed her to the plants in front of the window. "Look," her mother said, and Eileen saw that the violet had a lovely pink flower blooming from its middle.

"That's really nice, Mom."

"And there are more buds beside it, see?"

"Yeah."

This would be a gift, Eileen knew, these few moments with her mother and her plants, a short delay before the reminders of who they really were began again. So she asked her mother something about each plant, anything that would make the moment last.

"You should work with plants, Mom. I mean for a living."

"I probably wouldn't like it anymore if it was a job."

"What if you had your own shop?"

"You're a dreamer."

"Lots of people work doing things they love."

"Like singing?"

Eileen blushed, realizing her mother always knew her secret dreams. "You could have been a singer, I bet," Eileen said. Her mother turned her attention to her plants again.

"Could have been doesn't count. What counts is what

62

you are when you wake up every morning." The sadness had returned. Eileen felt it come out of hiding, change the quality of the air, the color of the light. She tried to think of some way to keep it away, something to say, do. But her mother had already closed up.

"You better find something to wear to church."

Eileen did as she was told.

By the time Neal and Eileen reached the park after mass, it had begun to drizzle, a fine mist that coated the air and thickened the sweet green smells of an almost spring. They found Liz only by chance. She was near her old blue Volkswagen parked on West Side Avenue, putting her guitar into her trunk. Neal ran to her, fearing they'd miss the chance to see her.

Liz said she'd looked for them all morning, hoping they'd show up early. "There's no money here today," she said. "I'm taking the day off." She opened the car and lowered herself into the driver's seat. Eileen didn't want her to go, realizing how eager she'd been to see her.

"You're g-going?" Neal said.

"I'm outta here," Liz said, finding a place for her legs, as if she were getting into a kiddie car. She turned the key, but the car ignored her.

"Where?" Neal said, leaning into the passenger window.

Liz looked at him, saw he was disappointed. "I don't really know." She was undecided, not sure what to do. She looked at both of them, then away. "There's a guy I owe a visit to."

No one said anything. She tried the car again. No response.

"What are you two doing?" Eileen thought Liz had come to some decision, so she shrugged, trying not to hope to be invited along.

"Have you guys ever seen Ellis Island?" They shook their heads. "Want to see it? We can get the ferry downtown. Check it out."

Eileen hesitated, mumbled something about not being sure what their plans were, but Liz had already reached over and opened the passenger door. Neal climbed into the back. Eileen waited only a beat or two, then got in, feeling scared and excited.

"Who needs guys anyway, right, Eileen?"

"Hey," Neal said.

"Present company excepted, of course," Liz said, winking at Eileen.

After a few more tries, the Volkswagen started and they headed downtown. Eileen had never been to that part of the city before. It was run-down, dirty, like most of the rest of the city. They followed the road that led to the park where the ferry was, a bumpy narrow strip lined with two-story buildings housing one unglamorous industry after another. The place was flat, desolate, altogether unremarkable, that is until the road turned sharply toward the park and there, almost shocking in their nearness, rose the shining, terrible buildings of downtown New York less than a mile across the water. Eileen had seen the New York skyline many times, mostly from a bus on the turnpike. Always lit, always distant, and deceptively serene. But this close, the buildings seemed unreal, as if the glass and concrete had been painted there as some ridiculous backdrop for this drab little park in this ugly little city.

Liz paid their fare for the ferry and the ride was glorious. The air on the water had a delicious chill. Liz talked about the island, about what they'd see there. She saw that they knew next to nothing about Ellis Island and seemed pleased with the chance to tell them what she knew. Eileen was content to let her think she was interested, but for all she cared, their trip could have begun and ended with this ferry ride and she'd have been thrilled enough.

But later, on the island, after the sheer bigness of it was done making its impression on her—the huge registry hall, the expansive ceiling with its elegant arches and countless tiny tiles, the half-circle windows rising like huge glowing suns from the tops of the walls—later the little details began to captivate her. The pictures, the passports, the unimposing possessions of restless, curious people who had come so far, crossed miles of ocean to this great uncozy place, their first stop in a land where they had no home.

The walls of one room had photos, taken mostly in their old countries, before they left for America. They must have treasured these, clung to them, arriving in a place where they had only the vaguest clues about the way you were supposed to do things, a foreign place. Eileen believed she knew that feeling. She had felt that way many times about the world outside her family. She often didn't understand the way things were supposed to be. She had only television and friends to go by. Friends never lasted because Eileen moved so much, and television seemed to be about rich families blowing ordinary events in their lives all out of proportion and calling them problems. How long did normal families have to save to buy shoes?

What did they do if there was no money for detergent that week?

She remembered her friend Amy in fourth grade. She'd gone shopping in the supermarket with Amy's family one Friday night, watched them buy everything they wanted. Everything. And Amy had said they did this every Friday night. Eileen remembered thinking that Amy must have been rich and shied away from her after that. Later she realized there were many kids whose families did this, kids who did not consider themselves rich or even lucky.

Eileen leaned forward, looked more closely at a large faded picture of a girl from Sligo, Ireland. A girl her age maybe. She wasn't sure. At least the girl was her size. She had long, straight, unruly hair and she was dressed in a white communion dress with a veil. Something about the girl was impressive. Not her looks. She was plain. No. It was the unshy, sure-of-herself look in her eyes that you didn't expect in someone so young. There was a bit of something royal in the way she stood there for the camera, one hand resting gently on a chair, something that told you she saw the fuss being made over her as entirely appropriate. No one in Eileen's family had ever taken a picture of just Eileen—by herself. With Deirdre. With Neal. With Deirdre and Neal. Stuck among a bunch of cousins on a couch. But never a photo taken specially of her. A girlfriend took one of her on a field trip once. It had come out with her forehead chopped off.

"Listen. I'm taking Neal outside. He's getting restless." Liz startled her.

"Outside?"

"Yeah. I'll show him the wall I told you about. With all the names on it."

"Oh. Okay."

"Find somebody you know?" Liz asked, motioning to the pictures. Eileen smiled. "Did you see Bridget and Formagh?"

"Who?"

"My great-aunt and uncle. Bridget and Formagh. Great-great, actually."

"Your relatives are in this exhibit?"

"I swear to God. Com'ere."

Liz took her across the room to a huge photo of a man and a woman who looked to be in their early sixties. The man was stiff, lean, and angular, in a Sunday-best suit, seated in a straight-back chair. He had a full white beard and lots of white hair, but no mustache. In spite of the formal pose, he seemed surprised about the whole business, a man unused to things outside his routines. Bridget was another matter. Bridget stood solidly beside him, looking as if she'd forced her bulk into her formal, two-piece Victorian suit the way she'd force her way through opposition of any kind. Her suit—which must have fit her once—was modest, but the look on her face was formidable, something a Dominican nun might put on for detention.

"There they are. My second cousins. Great-great-aunt Bridget and Uncle Formagh—twice removed."

"Removed from what?"

"Nowhere, silly. It means your cousin's relatives. These two were my third cousin's great-great-aunt and uncle."

"Get real," Eileen told her.

"I'm not kidding. Ask my sister Katie. I'll introduce you to her. In fact you won't have to ask her cause she looks just like Aunt Bridget. Katie's a meatpacker in the city."

Eileen laughed.

"You don't believe me, do you? I'll prove it to you. My mother's got a million old pictures of the family. She's even got one of Bridget at the seashore with a bathing suit and a parasol."

"Does your mother really have old pictures like this?"

"Of her whole family." Something in Liz's voice changed, and Eileen could tell she wasn't joking anymore. "She's the historian; everybody passed them down."

"What about your father?"

"C-c-come on, Liz," Neal called.

"My father." Liz paused, not sure how to say it. "Well, he ain't into family."

Eileen looked away, afraid she had touched on something too private.

"Listen, I gotta go. We'll be outside by the wall. I'll look McGuire up in the computer for you before I go out, see if any of your people are on there."

This was not the first time Eileen wished Liz knew her name.

10

There were two nines and an eight in Liz's phone number, so each time Eileen tried to call her she propped two pillows on each side of the phone and made a sort of tent, hoping she could stifle the sound of the dial. Her mom was in the living room, watching a rerun of "L.A. Law." Deirdre was putting laundry away, and Neal was protecting his cowboys from being ambushed by a band of Apaches in the hall.

There was still no answer. She had called her first at eight o'clock. She wasn't worried then, but now it was almost ten-thirty and a small fear like a lump was forming in her stomach. How could she have trusted her? She'd lose the ten dollars she gave her, lose her guitar, her lessons, lose her chance to be a famous singer.

She hardly remembered sleeping that night, haunted by the feeling that something was unfinished. She had not told her mom about her job yet and she couldn't give her the money she'd set aside, so they had peanut butter sandwiches for dinner. She felt guilty, believing she had no right to this secret. She vowed to call Liz as soon as she finished at Zeigler's. Then she'd tell her mother right away.

She never got the chance. When she got back to Zeigler's after her first round of deliveries, Deirdre was standing in front of Mr. Zeigler's fresh vegetables, trying to find the three biggest potatoes. Three big potatoes would mash for one night's supper plus some leftovers. Deirdre spotted her immediately, the way a lioness senses its own, but a huge split second of silence passed before Deirdre asked, "What are you doing here?" Her eyes narrowed, the mouth tensed. Suspicion was Deirdre's first and most comfortable response.

Eileen said nothing. "Answer me." Deirdre's voice rose, and Mr. Zeigler came out from behind the counter. He took a few steps toward them, then stopped. "Where did you get that bike out there?" Silence. "Where did you get the bike?"

"I gave her the bike," Zeigler said, confused. "She's doing a wonderful job."

Deirdre looked at Mr. Zeigler, then back to Eileen. "You're working here?" Eileen had no answer.

Deirdre's eyes darkened. "I need to talk to Eileen outside," she said to Mr. Zeigler. "Can she come outside with me?"

He nodded. Eileen hurried outside, closing her jacket around her. Deirdre handed Zeigler the three potatoes and followed. "How long have you been working here?"

"A week."

"What does he pay you?"

"I don't have to tell you that."

"No. You don't have to. And I don't have to give Mom

every dime I make when I baby-sit. Nobody has to do anything they don't want to."

"I'm not doing anything wrong."

"All you worry about is yourself."

"That's not true."

"You think you can get your own job and keep your money for yourself."

"I wasn't."

"Good. Then you can buy the stuff we need tonight. Here's the list."

Deirdre smacked the paper into Eileen's hand and left her there. Eileen watched her sister walk toward home with big angry steps, watched her till she turned down Merrick Street. Then Eileen leaned against Mr. Zeigler's window, looked across the street at the tavern her father used to drink in, remembered going in there with Deirdre to find out if he was coming home for dinner or whether he had money left for them to get something to eat. The bartender, Larry, had always looked at them sadly. "Get home with your kids," he'd say to her father. But he wasn't moving. Anyone could see that. And Larry would look at Deirdre and his face would soften, and something tender about his eyes would be meant only for her, and Eileen wondered if that's the way a person's face looked when he loved you. But he never looked at Eileen that way, and now she wondered—not for the first time—if there was something, not just a prettiness but a goodness, maybe, in Deirdre that made people love her. A goodness she just didn't have.

Deirdre was making hamburgers, and Mrs. McDonaugh was sitting at the table going through the mail. She looked angry. Eileen couldn't tell for sure if she was angry at her or just angry in general. Maybe Deirdre hadn't told her yet. She slipped the bag from Zeigler's onto the counter, mumbled a hello, and went back into the hall.

"Eileen," her mother called. "What took you so long? Did Zeigler give you a hard time?" Eileen returned to the doorway.

"No. I mean yes." Her mother took a look at her, alert for anything off cue.

"What's going on? What's that look on your face?"

Eileen glanced at Deirdre, but Deirdre kept to the hamburgers. "Nothing."

"Let's hear it."

"I mean nothing to worry about."

"Get on with it, Eileen."

"I've got a job."

Her mother couldn't seem to register this. Her face appeared stuck unwillingly in disapproval.

"What are you talking about?"

"Mr. Zeigler gave me a job at the store."

"Well . . . that's . . . well . . . How did that happen?"

"He needed somebody."

"Yes?"

"So he asked me to work for him."

"After school?"

"Yes."

"Every day?"

"No. Monday, Wednesday, and Friday. And he says he may need me on Saturday mornings, too."

"Well. That's fine. That's just fine. What are you doing?"

"I deliver groceries mostly. And clean the store a little. Unpack boxes. You know."

"What is he paying you?"

"Fifteen dollars."

"That doesn't seem like much for all that. Leave it to Zeigler to rip off a child."

"He lets me use his bike," Eileen said quickly. She was afraid her mother would call to scold him. She reached hurriedly into her pocket to give her mother what remained of her first week's pay. "Here," she said. "Here's the money right here. I had to take some out for the groceries." She laid the curled-up dollars and the loose change in the middle of the kitchen table. Her mother smiled—first at the money, then at Eileen.

"This is going to be a wonderful help, Eileen. You have no idea."

"Sure, Mom."

"Now, don't tell your father anything about this. All he needs is one more excuse not to send us money." She picked up the last of the dollars, uncurled them, looked at Eileen. "We can't do it this week, but maybe next time you can keep something for yourself." Eileen thought she heard Deirdre make a sound in her throat. Mrs. McDonaugh didn't notice it. There was an easiness about her mother now, an effortlessness in the way she moved away from the table, the way she talked. A confidence that came from the difference she believed fifteen dollars a week would make in their lives. She left them in the kitchen, went off to change to a house dress the way she did every night. And like every night, she'd settle in front of the television with a beer after dinner, and before long there'd be no way of telling from her face what the day had been like for her—or even any of the years.

"Fifteen dollars?" Deirdre said to Eileen. She didn't answer. "Better hope she never finds out."

Liz said, "I've got it right here," and Eileen dropped the receiver. She fished it back to her by its long, tangled cord and heard her call, "Leen, you there? Eileen?"

"I'm here." She was breathless, excited. She had waited till nine o'clock to call.

"So when's your first lesson?"

"How much was it?"

"I got him down to sixty-five dollars. It was no easy job."

"When does he want the money?"

"He'll take the installment plan."

Eileen squeaked a little.

"I thought you'd like that. So when do we start? I'm a very small operation. Got to keep cash flow moving."

Eileen hadn't really thought they'd ever start. "Gee, I don't know."

"Well, what time do you get home from school? I have a two o'clock class, but I could get to you by three-thirty."

"No. Not here. It can't be here." She said it too quickly, too forcefully.

Liz seemed confused after that. "Well, how do you want to work this?"

"I don't know. It's just too noisy here. All Neal's friends are always around after school. A full house, you know. And my sister blasts her stereo."

"Your sister? You got a sister?" Eileen pretended she hadn't heard the question.

"Where can we go?" she said.

"You can't come here. I've got an idea. The lit magazine has an office on Glenwood, right across from the college. I've got a key. We can go there if you don't mind lost poets wandering in now and then."

Mind. She was delighted. The thought of being on a college campus made her heart race. "I guess I could put up with that."

"Good. Wednesday?"

She had to work that day. "Can't. I'm going shopping with my mom."

"Are you sure you want to do this?"

"Yes. How about Thursday? I can always come on Thursdays. Or Tuesdays too."

"Okay. Thursday. Wait for me in front of one-twenty-five Glenwood at three-thirty."

"Okay."

"Did you call Dr. Margolin yet?"

Eileen hesitated. "I tried a couple of times. The line was busy."

"Well, bring Neal on Thursday. We'll take him over for a visit when we're done."

"I don't know."

"Does your mother think it's a bad idea?"

"No. No. She thinks it's a great idea."

"Good. Then bring him, Leen. She can help him a lot."

"Okay, I'll bring him."

"Good. Listen, I gotta run. I'll see ya Thursday," she said, and hung up, but Eileen held the receiver a long time after.

75

11

Meeting Dr. Margolin was not Neal's idea of a good time. He made that clear to Eileen, even threatening to spill the beans if Eileen didn't leave him alone about it. And there were a lot of beans to spill. He could tell his mother about the guitar and the lessons. He could even tell Liz that his mother didn't know anything about Dr. Margolin.

Eileen wasn't really afraid Neal would tell. It just wasn't in him. But she wasn't sure how she was going to get him to go to Margolin with her. And she felt that she *had* to now. She was afraid of what Liz would think if she didn't. And anyway, what reason could she give Liz for *not* taking him? "Oh, well, you see, my family doesn't want Neal to visit a therapist because my mother gets so angry at the very idea that Neal stutters that she pops her buttons, and, you see, my father's usually too drunk to notice. You understand."

So Eileen promised her brother she'd be his slave for two weeks. This was big-time bargaining. It meant doing all of his chores and even his homework and generally any silly thing he wanted without protest. But even this hadn't convinced him. What made the difference was Liz. "What am I going to tell her? She really wants you to go," she said to Neal, and that did the trick, because Eileen knew that in Neal's roster of people who count in the world, Liz now had first place. She read to him, she played ball with him, danced with him. And she never nagged.

Eileen didn't do very well at her first lesson. Liz encouraged her, but it didn't help. She felt stiff and awkward and nervous and just couldn't settle into it. When she told Liz she wanted to leave the guitar with her, she was sure Liz thought she wasn't really interested in learning, since she wouldn't be practicing. But Eileen wasn't ready to risk having her mother find out. When they were finished, they went outside and Liz played catch with Neal until it was time to visit Dr. Margolin.

Dr. Margolin's office was right down the street in an old three-family house converted to offices for the college. Liz took them up to the second floor. The sign under the peephole said DR. ROSALYN MARGOLIN, HOURS BY APPOINTMENT. Eileen found it strange to find desks and filing cabinets in what was once someone's living room. A boy came in from the kitchen to ask if he could help. He seemed especially interested in helping Liz. Neal was less uptight than Eileen expected. Maybe because the place was so unlike any kind of doctor's office.

A small dark woman came out of a door at the end of the hall that led away from the room they were in. Liz called to her, "Hey, Doc, how's it going?" The woman smiled, came toward them. She gave the papers she was

77

holding to the student and held her hands out to Liz. Liz took both of them in hers, and Eileen could tell they really liked each other.

"I never see you anymore," Dr. Margolin said.

"It's the price of stardom, Doc. I'm always on the move."

"Making money?"

"Things are happening."

"You've got dollars on the brain."

"What brain? Don't you remember my final?"

"Fondly." She looked down at Neal then, as if she'd known him just as long. "Are you Neal?" Neal nodded. "I'm glad you decided to come."

Neal stood a bit taller then, pleased that this grown-up assumed he had a part in the decision.

"This is Eileen," Liz said, "Neal's sister."

Dr. Margolin smiled. "Hello, Eileen." Her face was kind, capable. "Liz, we won't need you for a while. You can go check your stock listings or something."

Liz laughed. "See ya next time, Doc." She turned to Neal and said softly, "Don't talk her ear off, Jackson."

Liz left them and Dr. Margolin started right in. "Well, shall we talk about talking?" Eileen and Neal followed her down the hall to her office. Dr. Margolin sat with Neal on a couch, motioned Eileen to a nearby chair. She explained right off what stuttering was—and wasn't. There wasn't anything wrong with Neal, Dr. Margolin said. Stuttering was something he had gotten into the habit of doing and could learn not to do if he practiced some tools she could show him. The words helped something in Eileen to untangle, a knot that had formed a very long time ago.

The doctor said stuttering happened when you tried to force words out. She told them to imagine a door that you've opened easily many times before, but one day the door sticks. So you try to force it open. The problem is you never know from then on whether the door will open for you. Soon you're always afraid it won't open and you always try to force it.

Dr. Margolin talked to Neal for a long time, listened to him answer each question. Eileen listened, too, feeling embarrassed and sad for him. Such familiar feelings. Eileen saw that to Dr. Margolin things were unfolding as she expected, what she was finding was just what she needed to find, and mixed into it all was an expression of confidence—of certainty even—that she could make this go away. And in Eileen the guarded hope that had started with Dr. Margolin's smile became a conviction. A fairy godmother with a fountain pen for a wand had just proclaimed that things did not have to be this way.

More than once Dr. Margolin told Eileen to bring in her parents. Each time, Eileen dodged the request with an excuse about how they both worked and couldn't get away, and Dr. Margolin would ask a little more about things at home, until she told Neal to wait outside and got right to the point. "If your parents get angry about Neal's stuttering or haven't got the money or there's some other reason you think you can't tell me, use this form to get things started. All we need is one signature and I can get Neal into the state program with a reduced rate, but the application has to be filed by next week. If you want me to call your parents, I will. If you can do it yourself, that's better. But come back to me. I can help him."

Eileen nodded and made a silent promise to herself and to Neal that she would. No matter what.

The Saturday after Eileen's lesson, she visited her father with Neal and Deirdre. His tiny kitchen table was flush against the window, and Eileen leaned her forehead against the cloudy pane, thinking about her guitar, hardly aware of what the others were saying.

Neal sat on the floor, playing with some toy contraption that stretched the length of his arm, then wound around itself when he touched the trigger. It made a sharp, sudden noise when it sprang, and the rhythm of the sound was so regular that Eileen forgot about it until her Dad scolded him to stop. Neal joined her at the window, holding fists to his eyes to make binoculars.

Eileen told her father all about Dr. Margolin while he was still sober, though he didn't seem interested. Mr. McDonaugh had made up his mind long ago that Neal would outgrow his problem, but Eileen didn't think he'd resist getting him some help in the meantime.

When her father brought his coffee to the table, Eileen took the application form from her back pocket, unfolded it, and slipped it next to his cup. "All you have to do is sign that, Dad. There's nothing to fill out. Then they can start working with him."

He looked at the form. He was irritable. "What the hell is the Division of Health and Human Services? We some kind of charity case?"

"No, Dad. That's just . . ."

"They can shove it. Neal doesn't need their do-gooder bullshit. By the time he gets whiskers, he'll be over it."

"Dad, she said he needs to . . ."

80

"Your mother makes him a nervous wreck. That's the problem. He doesn't stutter around me."

"He doesn't talk around you," Deirdre said, and sat down at the table with them. Neal found a neutral corner.

"Let them get him out from under that bitch. Give *her* some therapy. There's your answer."

"He stutters with everybody, Dad," Deirdre said. "It's worse now than before." She kept her voice level.

He didn't argue. "Like I said. Your mother's got him crazy. Where we gonna go today?" he said to Deirdre.

"Anywhere but Gerrity's," she said.

"Uppity today, are you?"

Deirdre didn't answer.

"The place suits me fine. And we're going." His tone was stern. It looked as if he'd found a place for his anger to settle.

"I'm not," Deirdre said, and Eileen was afraid for her.

"What's up your nose?"

Deirdre didn't look at him.

"You got a problem with my friends?"

"N-n-" Eileen could see Neal was frightened, trying to speak.

"You don't know how to be friendly. That's what's wrong with you." Eileen wondered if Deirdre would say the words, tell him why she didn't want to be around those men anymore, tell the way they touched her, the things they whispered to her. But Deirdre just stared at him, so he leaned toward her. "What's your problem?" he said. "You too good for us anymore?"

"That's right." It was all he needed. He slapped her hard and she fell over, chair and all. Her face reddened; she was close to tears. Neal and Eileen stayed quiet. Their

81

father stood, pulled himself to his full height, and gave his trousers a great tug, as if he were satisfied with himself, but something about him had unraveled, some part of him that was afraid showed in his face and he moved away from them, stared out the window, breathing heavily.

Deirdre got up, put the chair upright. She was still trembling. "Wait for me outside," she told them.

Eileen grabbed their jackets and took Neal outside. She kept her ear to the door and heard what they said. "Guess you're pissed at your old man now," he said.

"Sign Neal's form," Deirdre told him. She sounded like a grown-up.

"You're still my girl, ain't you?"

"Get your hands off me."

Eileen wished she hadn't heard this. She was afraid for her sister, but even more afraid that she should help her, open the door, make him stop.

"You're getting all worked up over nothing. I lost my temper. That's all. Let's have a visit like we were supposed to."

"I don't want to visit with you. I don't want to be anywhere near you."

"You're upset about those guys in Gerrity's. They're just a bunch of cowboys. Pay no attention to them." Eileen recognized her father's tone of voice. This was the way he talked when he wanted to cancel out what you saw with your own eyes, when he wanted you to pretend something wasn't there.

"Sign the form."

"I'm not signing any form."

"Sign it or I'm not coming here anymore and neither are Eileen and Neal." Her father said something Eileen couldn't hear, then something moved across the floor, like a chair. And for a few moments there were no sounds at all.

The door opened and Eileen jumped away.

"Let's go," Deirdre said to them. She looked upset. There was a brownish red circle on her cheekbone, and Eileen didn't want to ask her whether he'd signed the form. She hoped Deirdre hadn't left it behind, because then she'd have to get another.

"Zipper up your jackets," Deirdre said to them when they got downstairs. She helped Neal with his, though he didn't need her to. Outside, she reached into her pocket to find change for the bus. She gave Neal his fare, then reached in again, but this time she took out the folded white form, handed it to Eileen.

"You still want this?" she said.

"Thanks for trying," Eileen said. "I ain't giving up. Maybe I'll ask Dr. Margolin to call Mom."

"You don't need Dr. Margolin. It's all signed."

Eileen smiled, and Deirdre looked as if this pleasure was what she'd been waiting for, because she laughed really hard, as if she was satisfied that she had done something very, very well.

12

The paperwork for Neal's therapy took more than a week to process, and by then Eileen had learned the chords to two songs. The blisters on her fingers from the first lesson had hardened a bit, making tiny calluses she was proud of. But the blisters opened again at her second lesson because she couldn't practice in between—at least not with her guitar. She had to leave that with Liz, pretending she had no time to practice. But alone at night she went over the chords again and again, moving her fingers in the air and strumming her tummy.

They sang together well past the lesson hour and Eileen forgot herself then, had long moments when she was not self-conscious about how she looked or what to say next. She watched Liz closely. Sometimes a vein in Liz's neck swelled as she sang and her skin would redden. She always wore a denim or a flannel shirt like a farm girl. She had lots of freckles on her hands, and now that the weather was warmer she rolled up her sleeves and Eileen could see the freckles covered her forearms too. She loved when Liz talked about herself, her friends, her schoolwork. But when Liz asked her about herself, Eileen felt as if she were made of cardboard, with a painted-on face. She had nothing she could share, nothing of her own to give her. So she sang her songs and told her lies.

They were sitting on Fleabag, the staff's nickname for the old couch Liz and her friend had rescued from the street. It was threadbare, lumpy, altogether unattractive, but better than the floor. Liz was tightening a string on Eileen's guitar. She was forever adjusting strings, rarely satisfied with a sound for very long.

"How did you learn the guitar?" Eileen asked her.

"Me? Oh, I picked it up myself mostly. Friends of mine show me stuff now and then."

"Didn't you have lessons?"

"I was only eight when I started. My uncle gave me an old guitar he picked up somewhere, only had five strings. We couldn't afford lessons. I figured it out as I went along."

Eileen was surprised at this, not so much by the idea of her family not having money, but at hearing her say so, like it was no big deal. She decided that it probably wasn't like that for Liz's family anymore, or she wouldn't talk about it so casually. "You play real well," Eileen said. "Did your uncle play?"

"Uncle Seamus?" Liz laughed. "All Seamus could play was the jug, just like my dear old dad." There was no mistaking the bitterness in Liz's voice, and Eileen wondered what it would be like if it turned out Liz was not one of them, the normal people, the Beth Colasurdo people who came from Cosby-show families. She imagined what she might say to Liz if she were someone whose parents didn't know how to be a family, people who drank because they lost their jobs, drank because they couldn't make their payments, because the world was against them, because they were against themselves.

"What do you mean 'play the jug'?"

"Well if you hold the mouth of a jug of whiskey to your lips and blow just the right way, you can get a tune out of it."

"I think I've seen that on TV."

"And my Uncle Seamus knew his way around a jug of whiskey better than any man I've met since."

Like my father, Eileen thought, but she couldn't make the words come. She imagined she knew how Neal must feel, struggling to get words past his lips, to make someone understand, knowing there's a way to say it, a way to connect, watching how easily others did it. But she couldn't make these words come, couldn't get them said.

"And what about you? Where'd you get that voice?"

"Oh, my mother sings. She's pretty good, actually."

"Your brother is some dancer. Does that come from your mother, too?"

"She likes to dance. Her whole family does. Whenever we get together, we dance. Other families do normal family things." Eileen sighed. "We dance."

"I haven't done any normal family things in quite a while."

"Does your mother really throw you out in the morning?"

"I wouldn't hang around anyway. We ain't exactly a family anymore."

Eileen was afraid to ask why, and Liz got quiet, started working at something by John Lennon.

"You know this one?"

"Yeah, it's pretty."

Liz looked at her. "I had a sister your age. Of course, she's not your age anymore."

"What happened to her?"

"She had to leave. When my stepfather left." Eileen wasn't sure she understood, and she wasn't sure she should ask. Maybe she didn't want to hear. No one had ever talked to her this way before. About important stuff. Stuff you don't tell just anybody.

"My real father died when I was eight. We were on our own for a couple of years; then my mother married Artie. Tightwad Artie. One time we had BLTs for supper without the lettuce. The price went up, so Artie wouldn't buy it." Liz stopped playing, sat back. "He had a daughter. She was only four when they moved in with us. Tina. I called her Tinkerbell 'cause she was so tiny. She grew up, but she stayed so small. I didn't like her much. Not in the beginning. I wasn't too crazy about the whole idea. But after a while me and Tina got along pretty good, a lot better than our parents did. She thought I hated her 'cause I wouldn't talk. I didn't talk to anybody, but she didn't know that. When I did get around to talking to her, she seemed to like what I had to say."

"You don't see her anymore?"

"She's in Florida. That's where they went when Artie left. She wrote me in the beginning. That was four years ago."

"Did you write back?"

"A couple of times. Then it just kind of ended. You know." Liz concentrated on the Lennon song; Eileen sang the parts she knew.

When it was done, Eileen said, "So you don't have a sister Katie packing meat in the city?"

87

Liz laughed. "No. Tina's the only kind of sister I ever had. Till you came along." Eileen liked that; she liked that very much. But she had no idea how to tell her. "Neal all ready for next week?"

Eileen knew she meant the therapy. "I guess so," she said. Dr. Margolin already had him penciled in for his first session.

She wished she could talk to Liz now about the speech therapy. It was going to cost twenty dollars a visit, the lowest rate possible. There was a waiting list for state-funded participants to get into the program, and if Neal couldn't attend, his place would be given to someone else. Eileen had only until Monday to tell her mother about all of this and to bring the money for the first visit. She needed help figuring this one out, but asking Liz would mean telling her things Eileen never wanted her to know.

Eileen got that now-or-never feeling that she had right before a fast ride starts, the feeling that you can't turn back. She had to talk to her mother today. Delaying any longer could lose Neal his place.

"Don't worry. He's psyched. He won't let anything stop him."

Except my mother, thought Eileen, and she got up for her jacket, knowing it was time for the ride to start.

"You want to come by the park Sunday?" Liz said. "Sing some songs with me?"

Eileen shrugged, though she had planned to come. She loved to sing with her. "I don't know," she said. "If I'm not doing anything else, I guess."

Eileen walked to the theater, eight long blocks away. She told herself there was nothing to dread. After all, they could help Neal; it was good news. But still she walked as slowly as she could, rehearsing the words.

Nick the usher recognized her and let her into the empty theater. They were between shows, and her mother was behind the candy stand, straightening Goobers. "What's wrong?" she said when she saw Eileen.

"Nothing. I just came by. That's all."

"Just came by?"

Eileen shrugged. Her mother was not convinced, but she said no more.

"How come you're working back here?"

"Joanie's sick. John's working the counter during the shows, but he's cleaning up inside now. I've got to fill in. You want Raisinets?" she whispered.

"Okay."

"So what happened?"

"Just want to tell you something."

She filled in packages of red licorice. Eileen sucked her Raisinets and worked up courage. "It's about Neal," she finally said.

Her mother stopped for a moment, frightened.

"There's nothing wrong," Eileen said right away.

"What is it, then?"

"It's about his speech. You know." Eileen had learned never to use the word stuttering with her mother.

"What about it?"

"They can fix it now. They have new methods."

"You can't fix what's wrong with Neal with a book."

"It's not a book. It's therapy. Speech therapy. A new kind."

"I know all about that stuff. He's not old enough yet."

"He is, Mom. They have kids as young as seven."

89

"Who's they?"

"The state program. I met the lady at the college who runs it, and she says she can do a lot for Neal."

"What lady? What are you talking about?"

"Her name is Dr. Margolin. She's a professor. She's real nice. We got him all signed up."

"All signed up? For what?"

"For the therapy. It's state funded. It won't even cost a lot."

"Just who do you think you are?"

"I just . . ."

"You leave Neal to me." Her mother stood up, a box of Goobers in her fist. "He's not going to be signed up for anything."

"But, Mom, he's already . . ."

"I take care of this family, and I don't need you telling strangers our business." Her mother shook a finger at her; the Goobers shook, too.

"All I did was . . ."

"You just get home. I don't ever want to hear another word about this again."

Eileen ran across the lobby, out into the street. She raced along, her arm outstretched, slamming the palm of her hand as hard as she could against the parking meters, the clang of the cold, empty metal resonating with an emptiness inside of her, and she welcomed the pain in her hand. Traffic was heavy on the avenue, and she didn't hear her mother calling, nearly screaming, tripping in her high heels. Her mother didn't catch up until Eileen stopped at a corner to cross. Her mother was out of breath, her face all moist from running.

"Eileen," she said, but Eileen didn't want to look at

her. Her mother put her hand on Eileen's shoulder, and the girl stiffened. She hated when her mother touched her; it made Eileen feel needy, like a child, something she had no permission to feel. "Walk with me. Come on." They walked together down a side street that was quieter. "I know you mean well, darlin', and I know how you feel. I feel it every time I look into his face. But you have to let me take care of this. This isn't for you to be doing. When the time comes, we'll look into it."

"But Dr. Margolin can help him now. She said so."

"She doesn't even know him."

"She does."

Her mother seemed struck by this, hurt.

"I took him to meet her."

That made her angry. "Well, she doesn't know him like I do," she said, "and he doesn't need anybody probing and picking at him."

"It's not like that. You don't know anything about it."

"I know quite a bit about it. A boy like Neal is sensitive. It's cruel to call such attention to it. No one is going to do that to him." Her voice broke. "When he was starting first grade and Daddy lost his job—the one at RoTech—and we had to move in with Grandma, remember?"

"Yes."

"I took him to the new school to register. All the kids were at tables in this huge cafeteria. It must have been wide as a city block. We waited a long time. I had the papers he needed and they had his records from kindergarten. I watched the woman doing our line process each kid. She'd make a point of asking each one his name, then she'd take out a big buff-colored card, make her marks on it, and smile at the mother.

"She got to us, with a line of people behind us a mile long and lines on both sides, and, of course, she asked Neal his name. And all I wanted for that boy, all I wanted in the whole world was for him to say his name. You know how the stuttering comes and goes, and I prayed this once let him speak like any other boy. Once. But his head jerked back and his face got all twisted, the way it does when it's really bad. He was trying so hard. I don't have to tell you the look that came over that woman's face. Like he could hurt her or something. It seemed like the whole damn room was waiting for him, waiting to see what kind of freak he was, until she said, 'That's all right, son,' trying to hurry us out of the way. But it wasn't all right. There was nothing right about it. Neal wouldn't budge. He didn't want to be let off the hook. He wanted to say his name."

She got quiet, then spoke in a stronger voice as if to show the memory that it couldn't get the better of her. "After that I spoke to the doctors at the clinic, and they said there was no point in starting any therapy until he was much older."

"Dr. Margolin says he's old enough now, Mom. They can do a lot, she said."

"Even if you believe this Margolin woman, that kind of thing costs money, Eileen."

"It's only twenty dollars a visit. Most people have to pay sixty dollars, at least."

"Eileen, where am I supposed to get another twenty dollars a week?"

"Well, you've got my fifteen dollars and I'll get the rest. I can work Saturdays for Zeigler."

"We need that fifteen dollars just to live. Do some

arithmetic. The rent. Food. The phone. It's more than we have. Month after month."

"Well, Daddy helps."

"We can't count on Daddy. There's no point in that."

Eileen didn't want to hear any more. "I'm sorry," she said. "Let's forget it."

"Don't be sorry," her mother said. "I know you mean well."

Her mother sent her home and Eileen walked slowly, counting the sidewalk lines, until she felt a kind of rhythm, ridding her mind of distractions, keeping away any thoughts that wouldn't help solve her problem, because she was determined to solve it. Nothing her mother had said had changed her mind. She could do it. She knew she could do it somehow.

13

By late afternoon, Eileen had made a deal with Zeigler to work a couple of hours on Saturday mornings for an extra five dollars. He insisted at first that he didn't need her because the weather was getting warmer and there were fewer deliveries on the weekends. He said he'd have to cut back on the Saturdays once the summer started. Eileen would worry about summer when it came.

Next on her list was Liz. She hopped a bus to Saint Peter's and found Liz still in the office, talking to some friends. The blond one, Phil, was with her. Liz looked as if she'd been crying.

"Eileen," she said, opening the office door.

"Who's this cutie?" one of the boys said. For a flicker of a second Eileen believed the boy might think she was pretty. She had looked into the mirror at herself many long secret times, thinking she saw something kind of pretty if she held her face a certain way, but no one else had ever pointed out anything of the kind. "Eat. You're just skin and bones." "Pull that mousy hair away from your face." "Stand up straight." She decided the boy was teasing her, rubbing in how plain she was.

"Watch out for Mat," someone said. "He likes 'em young."

"This is Eileen," Liz said. "She's the next Debbie Gibson."

Eileen wasn't that crazy about Gibson, but they seemed to think she was hot stuff, so she smiled.

"What's up, Leen?"

"Can I talk to you?"

"Sure." Liz stepped outside the office with her.

"Are you coming to Bill's tonight?" the blond one called to her.

"I told you no," she said, then closed the door and turned to Eileen. "So what's up?"

"I need a favor, I guess."

"What kind of favor?"

"The college is having a summer writing program for high school freshmen next year. And I want to go."

"I'm no help with syntax."

"It's for creative kind of writing."

"You write stories too?"

"I'm not very good, but my teachers tell me I should keep at it."

"Great."

"Except I don't have the money."

"Money for what?"

"The writing program."

"What about your mom?"

"She won't let me."

"She said no?"

"I didn't ask her."

"Ask her. I bet she'd be thrilled that you want to do something like that. Most kids just veg out all summer."

"Believe me, she would not be thrilled. She wants me to be a nurse. She says writers can't make a living."

"She's right about that. But you don't have to start making your living this summer."

"Besides, she wants me to go to camp all summer. She'd have a fit, really."

"So where do I come in?"

"Well, I thought if I started saving, I could get enough money together by the time the program starts. So maybe you could shorten my lessons to half an hour and take five dollars instead of ten dollars for a while."

"But you're doing really well. You should be playing more, not less."

"Oh, I am. I am. I'm taking my guitar home tonight and I'm going to practice every day for an hour."

"Good, but . . ."

"And then I thought maybe you could ask your friend to hold off on the guitar payments for a while. Just till I got a little saved."

"Wait a minute, Leen. This isn't the way you work a deal. We owe him five dollars a week. We can't bug out on him."

"But you know I wouldn't do that. I just need this favor. I need it so bad."

"I think you ought to ask your mother."

"So she can say no and forbid me to register? What's my English teacher going to say? She selected me special. Just me and four other kids. I'll be the only one who doesn't go."

"Leen, I really think your mother would be proud of you. Just tell her. I bet she thinks it's the greatest thing since polyester." Liz put on her jacket, as if the matter was settled. "You want a ride home?"

"I can get home myself."

Liz rolled her eyes and reached for the doorknob.

"So we have a deal?" Eileen said.

Liz hesitated. "I don't think so," she said. "Anyway. I'd have to talk to Phil."

"Phil. Yeah," Eileen said. "Let's leave it up to Phil." She was angry.

"Eileen, it was his guitar. He's the one you owe the money to."

"Seems to me good old Phil owes me and Neal a favor or two."

Liz looked at her, frowning. "Say what you mean. Don't jerk me around."

"You think me and Neal don't know what was in those bags? The ones that belong to all your forgetful friends?"

Liz closed her eyes, pulled her hair away from her face. "Come on down here," she said, and took Eileen into a small dark room that may once have been the super's office. There was a bare metal desk, a wobbly chair. Liz closed the door. The only light came through the holes in the window shade. It smelled of stale cigarette smoke and basement. Neither one sat down.

"I was wrong to do that. I'm sorry. I'm not doing it anymore. You know that. I told Phil right after that last time, with the girl. The girl with the dog."

Eileen didn't care about Liz being sorry. She didn't want an apology; she wanted money. "Does he pay you to do that?"

97

"No." Liz's voice went up, insulted. "I never wanted anything to do with it."

"Then why did you do it?"

"Because Phil . . . I can't explain. I have a hard time saying no."

"You're not having too much trouble today."

"I'm saying you should tell your mother. That's all."

"Would he pay you?"

Liz looked confused.

"To deliver the bags. Would he pay you if you asked him?"

"What are you saying?"

"I could help you with the bags and you could share the money with me."

Liz was angry. "Forget it, Eileen. Do you understand? I don't do that. We're never doing that."

Eileen wanted to tell her what the money was for, scream it at her, let Liz hear it, let the whole world hear it. But she couldn't say the words. Telling Liz about it would make it all the more real. At least here with Liz she had an escape, a place to pretend things were different. She couldn't give that up. She grabbed the door and ran. Liz called her, but she didn't turn back. She ran outside into the street, daring the traffic to stop her.

14

Eileen went to Deirdre. She knew she'd be at the Laundromat. Deirdre hated the Laundromat. She'd shove the clothes into a washer and get right back outside, away from the rows of noisy, trembling machines, the spilled powder, the people waiting blankly, the closeness. This time she'd taken her history book with her; there was a test the next day. She sat on the sidewalk, leaning against the storefront. Eileen slid down next to her, told her she'd come by to help.

"I thought you gave up on chores," Deirdre said. "Now that you're supporting the family, I mean."

"Who did the bathroom this week?"

"Don't tell me somebody showed you how?"

"I do it a lot."

"Save it, Eileen. You're up to no good."

"I'm up to something, but it's something good. It's for Neal."

"That therapy?"

"Did Mom tell you I talked to her about it?"

"I told you she'd flip." Deirdre studied a map of Africa.

"She's wrong, you know. He *is* old enough."

"Who knows? Maybe she's wrong. Maybe not."

"Will you try to change her mind, then?"

"No," Deirdre said, and flipped the page of her book.

"Why not? You just said she's wrong."

"I said maybe. About the age. Not about whether we can afford it."

"I fixed all that. I got the money. Most of it."

"I know you have the money."

"What do you mean?"

"How else could you afford guitar lessons?"

"How'd you know?"

"You're something else, Eileen. You think you've got everybody fooled."

"How did you find out?"

"Nobody works for five dollars a day, not even a fool like you. And you didn't get calluses on your fingers from doing housework, that's for sure."

Eileen was quiet. There was no point in defending herself, especially not if she wanted to convince Deirdre to help.

"Are you telling Mom?"

Deirdre got angry then. "I should. You know that? I really should. I almost did."

"So how come?"

"How come what?"

"How come you didn't?"

Deirdre slammed the book closed. "Who knows? Maybe I figure it doesn't matter a whole lot. It's not going to change anything one way or the other. If you want to grab something for yourself, maybe you should. Nobody's going to do it for you."

Eileen didn't say anything.

"You know Cecily Bertelsen?" Deirdre said.

"The one they call Birdseed?"

Deirdre nodded. "She's taking guitar lessons!" Eileen laughed. "The girl sings like an anemic chicken, and she wants a spot in the senior Spring Festival. She ought to put the money into driving lessons. She's a menace on the road."

"She's got a car?"

"Her brother's old Honda."

"What's she got to do with any of this?"

"Because it's not fair. That's all. It's not fair. Her family's got money and we don't, so we come up empty every time."

"But that's how I feel about Neal's therapy."

"That's different. There's nothing they can do for Neal."

"There is so!"

"If you're so sure, then use the money you're spending on guitar lessons."

"I don't have to. We can get the money. If you'll help me."

"Get real, Eileen. You don't want to do anything for Neal. Not if it means sacrificing anything of yours. It's always you first."

"We could ask Daddy." Deirdre rolled her eyes. "Maybe you could chip in some of your baby-sitting money."

"You're a piece of work."

"And if you talk to Mom, maybe she'd see things differently. She'll listen to you."

"Well, I'm not. I'm not getting into it with her."

"What's it take to convince you?"

"I'm not the one needs convincing. She does, and you're wasting your time."

"You don't care about Neal."

Deirdre pushed her hard, and Eileen landed sideways on the pavement, hurting her elbow. "You make me sick," said Deirdre, "you and your schemes. You think you can twist people around and put them where you want them. And it doesn't matter where they land as long as you come out on top."

"I'm just trying to help Neal."

"Nobody can help Neal. Don't you get it? You can't change who we are. And you can't change who you are. I don't care how many lessons you take."

"How can you stand it? Believing that?"

"Believe? What do you mean believe? This ain't a theory. It is what it is, staring you in the face."

"So you're just going to do nothing about it? About the way things are?"

Deirdre didn't answer right away. It was as if she had a secret, something she wasn't sure she should reveal. "Someday I'll just be gone," she said finally, her voice small, soft. She opened her book again, searching for her map. Eileen saw that Deirdre meant it, that someday she would leave them and that once she did, she'd never come back. This frightened Eileen, the idea that Deirdre saw no way to change things, no hope. Maybe Deirdre was right. Maybe it was better to close your eyes to it, close your whole self down until the day came when you could run away and finally be free. But Eileen was already sure what the waiting would do. That's what frightened her. The waiting would eat her up, nibble away at her until there was nothing left to set free.

Eileen got to her feet. "Maybe you're right," she said, but she wasn't sure Deirdre heard her. Deirdre had gone back inside, back to the rows of noisy machines, the rows of people waiting blankly.

Vinny was arranging the shoes on the counter when Eileen got to the shop. He turned at the tinkle of the entry bell, and the broad smile on his face made Eileen feel welcome but guilty. She hadn't come around in many weeks.

"Eileen. Good," he said. This was Vinny's telegraphic way of saying he was glad she was here and that she looked well.

"How's it going?" Eileen said.

"Good. Go good."

Eileen helped him finish the shoes, and there was nothing they needed to say for a time. When they were done, Vinny reversed the CLOSED sign on the door, and it was the world's turn to be open for business. Then he went behind the counter to tend to the cash register and Eileen perched herself on a shoe-shine seat. She wanted Vinny to see that something was bothering her.

"Thing wrong?" he asked her.

"You said it. Just about everything I can think of is wrong. A mess."

"Tomorrow good." Vinny always said that when she and Neal were upset. But it didn't seem to Eileen that anything was going to be good tomorrow or ever. It was all right to cry with Vinny. He didn't take it personally.

Eileen had learned that, and so when the sadness came real strong, she didn't push it down the way she did at home. She just cried.

Vinny stopped for a second, looked toward Eileen. "Someone hurt you?"

"No," Eileen sobbed. "No. I just can't get anybody to do what I want. I can never get anything I want—even when it isn't for me."

Vinny listened to her cry some more, didn't interrupt. Finally, he said, "Fix something."

"That's what I'm trying to do, and they won't listen to me. I can't fix it if they won't listen."

"No. Fix something. You be better."

Eileen had no idea what he was talking about. She tried again to make him understand. "Vinny, I'm trying to do something for Neal, something he needs real bad. But I can't get my mother to help me. She won't change her mind. Even my sister won't help me."

"No fix people. Fix shoes."

"What?"

"I fix. Fix shoes. No people." As he shrugged his shoulders, Eileen thought she understood him. It was useless to try to change people.

She came down from her perch. "Well, I can't fix people or shoes either."

"You fix," he said, pointing to the neat rows of shoes on the counter. "Feel good." Eileen saw that Vinny thought this would make her feel better, arranging the shoes on the counter for him the way she used to.

"That's okay, Vinny. You fixed them already. You did a good job."

But Vinny said again, "You fix. Feel good." And as he

104

pushed the shoes gently toward her side of the counter and heard some of them fall, a merry look was on his face. For a second Eileen didn't respond, just stared down at the boot and the boy's brown shoe at her feet. Then Vinny's big broad chuckle filled the little place, and Eileen pushed and tossed and slid all the rest of the shoes off the counter with him and laughed till she was crying again.

Vinny returned to his chores and let Eileen take care of the shoes. She did it slowly, with great care, taking pains to meet Vinny's exacting standards. She finished and felt better, seeing that taking care of this little piece of business made a difference somehow, not to the world perhaps but to the way she felt about it.

When Eileen was ready to leave, Vinny asked her to wait. "Thing for you," he said, and went quickly to his room. Eileen heard him move things around, then come out again. He was holding a small, delicate plane in his hands, a plane that looked exactly like Cloud Dancer— the same color, the same wings, the same smooth tiny stripe on its tail—but small enough to nestle in Vinny's huge palms.

"For you," he said, and placed it in her hands. It felt to Eileen like a bird just born.

15

When Liz found Eileen, it was almost eight-thirty and she'd been driving around for nearly an hour. Eileen was in Lincoln Park, sitting on the ground, leaning against a tree by the lake. Liz had gone this way only as a shortcut to West Side Avenue, never dreaming Eileen would be alone in the park after dark. The road wound around the lake, and Liz slammed on her brakes when she saw her. Eileen heard the car but didn't recognize it, only saw someone running toward her and got to her feet as fast as she could, ran for all she was worth in any direction but her pursuer's. Liz called her name, but all Eileen heard was the pounding of her own heart and the trees astir from a wind that would bring a strong spring rain. Liz had to tackle her to get her down.

"At least you had the sense to run," she said once she had her pinned. "What the hell are you doing in this park alone at night? You crazy or something?"

"Let me go."

"I might."

Eileen felt small, powerless. And she didn't like it. "Just get off me."

"Not until I get some answers."

Eileen was getting scared. She'd never seen Liz so angry before.

"What's your last name?"

"McGuire. I told you." Eileen felt a raindrop on her forehead.

"Tell me your name."

"What difference does it make what my name is?"

"Your sister goes to Snyder, doesn't she?"

Eileen looked past her, up into the dark, threatening sky.

"Where have you been all night?"

"I don't have to report to you. It's none of your business where I go."

"Why were you jerking me around? What was that business about at the office today? What do you need money for?"

"It doesn't matter. Just let me go."

"Are you doing drugs or something?"

"No. Jeez."

Liz eased off and let her up but kept her next to her on the grass.

"Your sister came looking for you at the office tonight. She's worried. Thinks you're going to do something crazy—like what I don't know—but something."

Eileen moaned. "She came to see you? What did she tell you?"

"Not a whole lot. Except that you deliver groceries for the German deli. We went there looking for you. They were closed, but we went up to their apartment. Now the old man's worried, too."

"A regular all-points bulletin. Where's Deirdre now?"

"I took her home. She didn't want your mother to get suspicious."

The thought of Liz seeing where they lived made her want to run. "Let me go. I've got to get home."

But Liz made Eileen face her. "Eileen, talk to me. What's all this about? Why were you pretending?"

Eileen slipped free and stood up. She felt angry all over again. Angry that Liz should know her secrets, hurt that she'd seen the kind of family she had. "I had a plan to rip you off for the guitar, okay?"

Liz didn't answer her, just sat there, and Eileen turned away from her into the darkness toward a path lit weakly by old streetlights. She went a long way, all tightened up in her anger until she felt the rain on her face, steady now. Ahead, a streetlight lit the mist; beyond that was darkness again. She stopped in the light, felt something loosen inside of her. She was afraid and didn't want to be alone anymore, not just alone in the dark but alone in herself with no one to know who she was. She looked back but couldn't see Liz. She called her name, then ran back down the path, panicky that it might be too late.

"I'm here. I'm here," Liz said. Eileen caught her breath, relieved to see her. Liz took her hand. "I figured you'd chicken out. Come on in the car."

They crossed the field quickly, got into the car. The rain came down hard, pounding the little Volkswagen roof, the wind threatening to lift it away. They were quiet at first, letting the rain make all the sounds. Liz leaned her head back, let herself sink into the seat. "You didn't have me fooled for a minute. I knew it from the first day."

"Knew what?" Eileen was afraid she was leading to something, something that would force her to be real.

"What you needed the money for."

"What?" Eileen was almost hoping Liz would guess right, so she could know it—everything—without her having to say the words.

"You're saving to buy me that suit."

"What suit?"

"The management consulting suit." Liz turned the car on. Eileen was afraid they were leaving, that her chance to talk to her was over, but Liz began to switch stations on the radio. Nothing pleased her long. The radio static and the bits of song annoyed Eileen; they seemed an interference. She let herself believe at first that she didn't know what they were getting in the way of, but she did. She wanted to talk to Liz; she wanted to be heard.

"Could we turn that off?" she said.

"Sure," Liz said, and snapped the radio knob. The silence was like a dare. She thought Liz would make it easy for her, ask her questions, but she didn't, and the words and the need to say them gathered in her throat until they hurt. She wanted to open the window, let the rain wash the tension away.

"My name is McDonaugh," she said, and with the sound of her name felt rescued, freed from the need to pretend. She began to talk, at first to the windshield, unable to look at Liz. She talked about how she'd gotten the money for the lessons and the guitar, about the way her parents reacted to the therapy for Neal. She told her

109

about her family, about who they were and who she wished they could be, about what it felt like to want things so badly.

When she finally looked over at Liz, she saw that she was not embarrassed by any of this, not wishing she were somewhere else. And Eileen felt safe, not only from the rain and the darkness and the dangerous park, but safe to be herself, free from the terrible consequences she had believed the truth would bring. Liz was not rejecting Eileen McDonaugh; only Eileen McGuire had done that.

"Families are weird," Liz said. "We have to live with these people and we don't even get to vote on who they're going to be. Sometimes they just land on us, like Tina and Artie did. What a family that was. These people weren't even related to me, really. And all of a sudden my bookshelf gets replaced by a toy chest and there's a bald guy where I used to sit for dinner.

"In the end I could see they were breaking up. Long before Tina could, I mean. And something started happening to me. Something crazy. I didn't want to be around Tina anymore. I stopped taking her anywhere, hardly talked to her. I stayed away from the house. She asked me once if I was mad at her and I acted like a jerk, told her I didn't care much about her one way or the other. The truth of it was I knew I was going to lose her and I couldn't stand it. She was the only person who ever thought I was important."

"I think you're important," Eileen said. "So does Neal."

"And you're important to me," she said, and they watched the rain because they were embarrassed.

"How does it look for Neal's therapy?" Liz said.

110

Eileen told her she'd lost hope for getting him into it, that she couldn't convince Deirdre to help her. "Want some free advice from a woman of the world?" Liz asked her.

"Is she in the backseat?"

"I'm talking about Liz C. O'Leary. Right here."

"I'll hear you out. On one condition."

"Shoot."

"You tell me what the *C* stands for?"

"You just get the words of wisdom, no extras."

"We'll see."

"Have Dr. Margolin call your mother. That's what will do it. You've got to remember that to your mother, you're a kid. She's not going to listen to a kid when it comes to this kind of thing."

"What would I say to her?"

"Who, Margolin?"

Eileen nodded. "Just be honest. Say you need her help." Eileen wasn't sure she liked this.

"And tell your mom you'll pay for the therapy. All of it."

"How?"

"By making a deal with me."

"I thought you said no more deals."

"I'm talking about an honest agreement where everybody knows the terms and what they're for. I'll take care of the guitar payments with Phil and I won't charge you for your lessons for a while." Eileen was too happy to speak. "If."

"If? What's the if?"

"This is a deal, remember? And the if is you come to the park with me on Sundays and sing."

111

"Sing? What for?"

"For the profits. I made twice as much that day you sang with me. The crowd loved it."

"I'd be scared."

"But you'd love it."

And Eileen smiled, because there was no fooling Liz—not anymore.

"We better get you home."

"My mother's going to kill me."

"That's all right. Maybe you'll come back in another life. As a rich management consultant."

"But she's going to be so mad. About everything, the lessons, the therapy, the works."

"What did you do that was so bad? You wanted guitar lessons, so you got a job and paid for them. You want to help your brother. Kids get medals for stuff like that."

"Not in my family. You can't go off and do something for yourself just because you want it." Liz let her finish. "Deirdre says I'm selfish. Maybe she's right. Maybe I ought to just wise up."

"It's not wrong to want something. I don't care what family you're in. It's only wrong to play games with people to get it. You need to believe in yourself, that's all." Liz turned the key in the ignition but got no response. "So does this motor." After the third try, it started.

"Could we stop by the office first?" Eileen asked.

"What for?"

"I want to get my guitar and practice for Sunday."

"At your service."

They drove toward the college, and Eileen listened to the sound the cars made in the wet streets as they moved through the rain. Streetlights took Liz's face in and out of the shadows, and the face Eileen saw was not the same one she remembered from that first day in the park. Liz looked relaxed, at ease, and Eileen saw that they both had changed. A tune would come into Liz's head and she'd sing a few lines, tap the beat on the steering wheel at the traffic light, then turn to Eileen and wink or grin. And Eileen wondered if this way of being with a person, this free, unburdened way, could be what family was supposed to mean. She wondered if your family had to be the one you're born into, if maybe you could build one instead, choosing one by one the people who made you feel good about yourself.

"Is it Constance?"

"No."

"Cora?"

"No."

"Clarabelle?"

"Forget it."

"Cassandra, that's it."

16

As Liz pulled up to Eileen's building, Eileen could see the faint dancing light from the TV screen in the living room window. The room she shared with Deirdre was brightly lit and she could see Deirdre's silhouette.

"Let me walk you inside. It's late," Liz said.

Eileen rolled her eyes, "I know my way."

"Humor me. I just want to make sure you're safe."

"All the servants have retired for the night."

"I'm not expecting to come in."

Liz followed her up the stoop. Eileen held her guitar under her jacket to protect it from the rain, had the tiny Cloud Dancer in her pocket. Inside, the hallway looked darker than usual to Eileen, dirtier. She watched Liz look around and felt responsible for it.

"Hallways like this are great for singing, you know. It's closed off with high ceilings. Listen." And she sang something by the Beatles, a song about a blackbird and learning to fly. The place changed then. The sounds made it special. Eileen joined in, and it was effortless. The sounds filled the place and came right back to them. The door at the top of the stairs opened and Deirdre came out, closing it softly behind her. She sat at the top of the stairs and smiled at their song. When they finished, she clapped for them. "You two are really good."

They laughed. "Are you okay?" Deirdre asked Eileen.

"Fine," Eileen said. "Is Mom mad?"

"She thinks you ate at Karen's."

"I better get upstairs."

"If she asks, tell her I'm at Mary's."

"Okay," Eileen said. Deirdre thanked Liz and left them.

Eileen watched her sister through the thick glass door. She moved slowly down the stoop, not seeming to notice the rain.

"I guess I'll see you Sunday. Okay, Clementine?"

"Okay," said Liz.

Upstairs the sound of Neal's police car siren came from his room, mixing with the serious voices of the real-life drama on TV. Eileen walked straight to the living room, afraid that hesitating would keep her from ever going in. She stood in the middle of the room, still wet, still determined, her guitar still under her jacket. The TV light played on her mother's face, bright, then dim, then brighter still, in unpredictable patterns of whiteness and shadow. Mrs. McDonaugh turned toward Eileen, but slowly, absently, as if drawn back without choice to the random light.

"You're home. Good," she said.

"Yes."

Satisfied, her mother turned back to the screen.

"You had dinner at Karen's."

"I didn't go to Karen's," Eileen said, but her mother wasn't listening.

Eileen flipped on the ceiling light and turned off the TV. Mrs. McDonaugh squinted from the glare, seemed confused.

"I said I didn't go to Karen's."

"I don't understand. Where were you, then?"

"I was getting the rest of the money for Neal's therapy."

Mrs. McDonaugh looked away, back at the empty gray screen, sipped her coffee.

"I took care of everything," Eileen told her.

Her mother got up. "We're not going to talk about that now," she said, and turned the TV back on. A soft electrical puff filled the screen with light again, a man's voice talked the meaningful talk that people share on TV— every word, every look making a connection, every question answered.

"We're not?" Eileen said, angry, but her mother was already back in her chair, somewhere else, out of reach. Eileen was jealous of this escape, this place she had where no one else could follow.

"Well, I am. I'm going to talk about it."

Her mother faced her, not sure she'd heard her right.

"What's that?" Mrs. McDonaugh said. She meant the guitar.

"It's mine."

"Who gave it to you?"

"I bought it. With my own money."

"What do you mean your own money?"

"I earned it and I bought it."

"You mean the money from the store?"

"Yes."

"How did you . . . ? You lied to me? About what Zeigler pays you?"

"I gave you . . ."

"How could you do such a thing? When you know we need every . . ."

"What about what I need?"

"I'm doing the best I can. How can . . . ?"

"No you're not, Ma. Not for me, you're not. And not for Neal. You want to pretend they can't do anything for Neal because he makes you feel guilty. That's why. You don't want to know what they can do."

"Guilty? Go talk to your father about guilt. He's the one who left us. What thanks do I get for not running out on you like he did?" Her face looked hard, and Eileen could see how trapped her mother was, caught in a life she'd never wanted.

"Mom, I'm sorry I lied. I'm sorry I had to lie. I didn't do anything wrong. You and Daddy, whatever happened, it's not my fault. I feel like I'm being punished for things I didn't do. You and Daddy did it. Not me." Eileen waited, a little shocked at what she'd said, expecting her mother to blow up. But she had sunk back into herself, sat with her head in her hands. "I earned this money, Mom. I earned this guitar and it's mine."

Mrs. McDonaugh sat motionless. She looked lost and alone. For a second, Eileen thought about telling her mother she'd take the guitar back, stop the lessons, anything to comfort her, but the words wouldn't come, because Eileen knew that her mother's unhappiness was not about a guitar; not about this night, but about all the nights before and all the nights ahead of her, repeating and repeating like a phonograph needle stuck in a single groove. Eileen could think of nothing to say that would make a difference. She flipped the light off, left her mother in the dark.

In her room, she laid the guitar case across her bed, put Cloud Dancer on the nightstand, and let her wet jacket drop to the floor. She flipped open the lid of the case, and the voice of the instrument echoed softly in the smooth, curved wood as she removed it. She sat down on the bed, placed the guitar on her lap, and leaned into it, moving her fingers along the strings. Then she heard the electrical puff of the TV again, the voices silenced this time, her mother's slow, heavy footsteps coming toward her room. Her mother reached the doorway and stood there, quiet. Eileen would not look up.

"You're learning how to play it?"

"Yes."

Mrs. McDonaugh's face softened, her eyes filled with tears the way they did when Eileen used to give her those Mother's Day trivets made out of ice-cream sticks.

"Can you sing me a song?"

Eileen hesitated, but only a little. "Yeah, sure I can," she said, but she didn't know what to sing. Her mother sat down on the bed, and Eileen smelled her perfume, the same one she'd used forever, the one made of wildflowers and sunrise. Then she remembered it, that old Irish song. Her mother would sing it to her over and over, but not since she was little and hurting, not since the times she still allowed her mother to hold her. It was a simple song, lonesome, about someone leaving, going far across the sea. It would only take three or four chords. She tried

118

them, holding the frets as tightly as she could, wanting the truest sounds she could make.

Eileen repeated the melody in her head a time or two, then started to sing, but her voice was off-key because of the tightness in her throat. She lost her bearings, got embarrassed, until her mother joined in, helping her find the place her voice belonged. They sang it through once, then once again, and Eileen didn't question why her mother wanted this, didn't dare to hope she'd want it again. She just let the song happen, let her mother's voice show hers where to go, a delicate harmony, maybe too fragile to last. Their song wasn't nearly as beautiful as it felt, but her mother's voice was deep and sure, and something about it made Eileen feel quiet inside. She glanced at Cloud Dancer on the nightstand, thought about Vinny's hands, his big, deliberate hands, his patience. Tomorrow she would ask Dr. Margolin to call her mother. Tomorrow she would try again to fix things.